Santa's Last Ride

Santa's Last Ride

JAMES SCHMITT AND MAGGIE MCCOY

atmosphere press

To my family for their support: my wife, Rebecca, for her belief in me and the book, especially at those times when I lost it; my kids, Matt and Sarah, for just being you – I could never have done it without you guys. To Maggie who believed my short story could be more.

To my husband, Mark, who put up with so many readings, of so many versions, for so many years; and especially to my brother, Jim, who gave me the opportunity to imagine life at the North Pole.

To the cherished memory of Dennis McCoy, our family's one true Santa Claus.

Chapter 1

Peering down from the loft in the barn, Kristy could just see her brother below. Peeking out from his ragged barn jacket lay his neck – bare and calling to her, but the target was not in range yet. She pulled back slowly, quietly from the edge. By shifting the shovel, most of its weight rested on the railing. While she waited for Chris to approach the drop zone, she checked her ammunition – a grey-green blob of moist, smelly moss that made Chris's nose wrinkle up in disgust.

Better and better.

The field elves around her began to giggle through their fingers. She frowned at them to keep quiet. At this time of the year, excitement was high at the North Pole, and it was hard for anyone to keep quiet for long.

The elves below were laughing too. Kristy knew that they were in on the joke. Kristy wished she shared the elves' way they spoke to each other without words. Below in the milling herd, Santa added his hearty ho, ho, ho's. She loved to play these jokes on her family and the elves, but mostly on her brother.

Kristy chanced another quick peek down. Chris was nearly in the center of the manger now. His head bent over his task of spreading feed out for the reindeer.

Good! He's not on to me.

She eyed the distance and her target's speed, took aim...

Fire!

A satisfying plop, followed by her brother's scream proved that her mission had been a success. She saw field elves laughing into their hands. Kristy roared and nearly fell out of the loft onto her sputtering brother who was frantically waving his hands and screaming for someone to come and get it off. Jumping around only made the moss slide down his shirt all the faster, which made Kristy laugh all the harder. Her sides ached. Laughter sprayed white clouds like dragons' breath around the icy barn.

She heard her father, Santa Claus, trying to stifle ho, ho ho's. Kristy hung onto the railing and laughed, knowing her father was in too good a mood this close to Christmas to scold her for her little gag. He chuckled as he came to Chris's rescue and began to brush off the moss. Like everyone in the barn, Santa was dressed in overalls, boots, a stocking cap, and a worn faded-red jacket. His overalls just fit more snuggly about the middle than anyone else's, except maybe for Sam, the head field elf.

"Is that any way to treat the next Santa?" Sam called up to Kristy.

"He's not Santa yet. He's just my stupid brother."

"Who's stupid?" Chris shouted up at her.

"Not me."

"Well, who gets the best grades?"

"That's only because Mom likes you best."

"I am sure that is not true," Santa said sternly, but the twinkle in his eyes took the edge off.

"Reindeer poop," Kristy replied, though she didn't really believe it herself.

"Language, young lady, language."

Chris shook his fist at her from behind their father's back.

"Listen, all of you. I realize it is a very short time until Christmas Eve and we are all getting excited and anxious. It has been a long season of very hard work, but the end is in sight. Tricks, gags, and practical jokes are well and good in their place, but we still have work to do here. I need you to get at it. The reindeer will not feed themselves."

As this last phrase left Santa's mouth, Chris exactly mimed the very same six words. Words heard time and again, day after day, year after year by their father and often their mother as well. Kristy snickered.

"I'll get you for this," Chris said pulling pieces of moss out of his hair.

"This seems to happen to you an awful lot," Santa mused. "Perhaps if the two of you changed places once in a while you could pay your sister back. She would learn a lesson and stop bugging you."

"Thanks, Dad, but we have a system worked out and it suits us just fine," Chris said. Then he went back to his work.

Kristy knew her father was satisfied when he slapped Chris on the arm before heading toward the stairs to the loft.

Kristy looked down at her brother for a moment and

paused. Something in Chris's tone of voice made her wonder if there was more to it. True, they had a system where she went up to the loft and threw down the feed for her brother to spread around the manger. She could not remember a time when they had done it differently, when he had climbed into the loft, and she waited below.

Behind Kristy, Santa's boots tromped loudly up the stairs. She shook those thoughts from her head.

Reindeer poop! I better get back to work.

Down below it was Chris's turn to laugh. She thought he was looking forward to her scolding.

Santa set down his lantern. Two colorful balls of light, called elvlight, left the lamp and drifted up to merge their lights with others in the dome above. Santa grabbed a pitchfork and joined Kristy at the edge.

"Move over, give me some room," Santa barked, but his eyes held an impish spark. He scooped up a heavy forkful of feed with a loud grunt. "I have had enough. It is time to quit fooling around. The herd must be fed and the *Naughty or Nice Book* still needs your attention.

"Now this is a shovelful, nothing like those little girly ones of yours," he boasted, and his grin was a challenge aimed at her.

Kristy knew this was more than just her father's jokester side coming out. He had done this to her before. He was trying to get her riled into having a shoveling duel with him so that she would work harder, but she couldn't help herself. He had called her "girly."

Kristy smiled back at her father, with what she hoped was her most evil smile. Then she dug her shovel deep into the moss - not taking her eyes off him. She did not want to end up like her brother with a head full of reindeer food.

"Let's just see who the Boss of the Moss really is," she said.

They gave each other their cheesiest pro-wrestler grimaces before flipping their loads over, dumping the feed into the manger below. As soon as they were emptied, Santa refilled his fork, Kristy her shovel, and they hurled moss down over the railing as fast as they could. Soon they were laughing together as the moss flew over the edge into the manger. Bits of feed floating around in the breeze they made attached to their hats and clothes.

Before Kristy gave out, her father stopped, grabbed her arm to halt her in mid-shovel and peered anxiously over the edge. Following his example, Kristy peered over too. All she saw was a mountain of moss tilted to the right in the manger below.

Chris isn't keeping up with us. He should have spread the feed out toward the reindeer by now.

Then she saw the look on her father's face. He was staring and turning white.

"Stay here," he ordered pushing her back from the edge, "don't move a muscle."

Santa vaulted over the railing. Shocked, Kristy ran back to watch him drop. He jumped to the low side of the mountain and landed with a hard thump – and a low moan. She could see he was in pain, but it didn't stop him.

"Chris, Chris," he called frantically as he tore into the pile of feed with mittened hands. "I'm coming Chris! Hold on! Take shallow breaths. I'm coming!"

Kristy grabbed hold of the rail to stay upright. First,

she felt weak and scared, and then all the lights, colors and sounds around her grew bright and sharp. There was a tingling in her arms and legs. She could not stand still. She had to do something - anything. She bolted down the stairs and tripped over Chris who was rolling on the floor in silent laughter.

Kristy's joy at finding her brother alive and well switched to anger. All the tingling pumping through her blood settled in her fists, which she used to smack Chris's head and shoulders. For good measure, she also kicked him with moss-covered boots. This had no effect on him. He continued to laugh as he raced around the reindeer toward the door.

Her dad was on the far side of the manger and only saw Chris as he reached the door. Kristy saw relief on his face as he slapped a hand on his chest and let out a great sigh. Santa flopped onto the moss and let his head fall back.

"Glad you two enjoyed that little contest," shouted Chris, with far too much joy. "Here's another one for you! The one who can spread this feed out the fastest is the Manger Master!"

Before he closed the door behind him, Chris quietly added, "I'll let you guys finish up here and I'll hit the Book! You keep reminding me the *Naughty or Nice Book* needs my attention."

Before either Santa or Kristy could protest, Chris bolted out the inner door and down the tunnel toward the library.

"He's off again," Kristy said. She felt frustrated that Chris got her back for her prank and angry that Chris's little trick scared her and hurt their dad.

One look at his face said it all. Everything above his beard was red and he was chewing his mustache.

I wouldn't want to be in Chris's shoes when Dad catches up with him.

Santa grabbed the shovel Chris had left behind and used it to help himself up from the moss. He groaned with pain as he moved. Kristy shuddered in sympathy and ran to help him stand.

"Are you okay, Dad?"

"I'll be all right, just give me a minute." He looked worried.

Without realizing what she was doing, Kristy now chewed her lip in concern. Sam and several of his helper elves jumped into the manger to help Santa to a seat.

"Sorry, honey," Santa said, "but I am in a great deal of pain here."

"What can I do for you?"

Santa patted her hand where it rested on his arm, "I will be fine in a minute. Just get on with the feeding. The elves will take my place and," he added sharply, "your brother's. I'll rest a bit, then bundle up and take the shortcut to the kitchen."

Kristy took the shovel in silence and began heaving and pushing the food to the edge, toward the waiting reindeer, while Santa rested on a bench near the outside door. With Sam's aid, he began to dress for the cold. By the time she finished spreading the feed to the edge of the manger and hung her overalls and barn jacket on a hook, he had gone.

Sighing, Kristy looked about her. She sensed the reindeer were happy to be eating and circling the manger. The elves wandered among them speaking softly, petting, patting, and reassuring.

Why am I always left here doing all the work? And Chris takes off?

She knew it was not Chris's favorite place to be, but it should be. It did not make her angry - all the work she put in here. She loved the reindeer after all, but she did wonder.

Why isn't Chris doing this? As the next Santa, this should be his job.

"Boys - I'll never get them," she said, and then she laughed. Her audience seemed to agree with her. The elves were all chuckling. She knew they had a hard time figuring out why any human did what they did. The reindeer had that certain cheerful look in their eyes that Kristy thought meant *fun*. They, of course, were all girls. What would they know about boys?

Kristy gathered the remaining lamps, two elvight in each, to take with her into the passage. She left the herd in peace and quiet as the dust settled in the low light.

Chapter 2

His nose hair had frozen together, and ice had formed in his mustache and beard. Snow crunched with each step of his boot. Behind him, Sam, with his short elfin legs, struggled to keep up.

Santa concentrated on each footfall. He took great care to plant each boot firmly before he made another move. It would not do to slip or slide, and heaven help him if he fell. Santa pictured himself pitched over in a drift, flat on his back, arms and legs flailing like an overturned ladybug.

It would take half a team of reindeer and half a dozen elves to get me upright. The indignity!

He chuckled at the thought. No, it would not do to injure himself just days before Christmas.

"Should I send for help from Medical?" Sam asked between huffs of icy breath, "you hit the ground pretty hard back there."

"That is not necessary," Santa chuckled, "but if there is an earthquake in Canada tomorrow, we will know why."

Sam, a dignified elf, was too serious to laugh.

"Santa, you are not as young as you used to be."

"Ja, but Sam I feel old. I have ever since the sleigh accident five years ago."

"You know, the elder Claus would have wedged up the sleigh tighter when sharpening the runners."

"Papa made mistakes too."

Sam frowned, "I know, but not as bad as that one. You were pinned to the shed floor for forty-five minutes before we freed you."

"My back has never fully recovered. In fact, it has gotten worse with the passing years. I am in an agony of burning pain – after only half an hour! It is a good thing Kristy was on hand to finish up the chores that my son should be doing.

"My kids," Santa complained as he reached the kitchen door. His frustration pushed him to grab the knob too quickly and his comment ended on a moan as his back twisted into sharp, stabbing pain.

Mrs. Claus opened the door with a warm, welcoming smile nestled in her plump face. Soft light haloed her where she stood. An aroma of fresh baked bread and hot cocoa wafted toward Santa as, gently but firmly, his wife and Sam led him to a chair.

"Thanks, Sam," Mrs. Claus said.

"My pleasure," Sam replied. He bowed and walked back out of the door toward the barn.

"My good glory, Papa, but you finished quickly to-night." Emma removed his parka and two layers of insulating clothing, settled him in a chair, and placed an ice pack on his back. Before he had a chance to thank her, she set a cup of steaming hot cocoa before him and, beside that, a slab of warm, buttered bread. She even had time to let the elvight out of the lamp and into the oven where the tiny creatures added their heat and light to that of their brothers and sisters amid delicate squeals of joy.

"I left Kristy, without Christopher again, to finish feeding the reindeer," Santa explained. "Emma, I can't keep this up any longer. I need to retire. It is just too hard on my back."

Emma leaned over, patted her husband's shoulder, and said, "You have been telling me this for years now Kris."

"Ja, I know. But this year must be my last run with the presents." He sighed, refilled his mug with hot cocoa, and grabbed a soft, warm sugar cookie. "I'll take Christopher with me this Christmas Eve and show him the ropes."

Frowning, Emma said, "Do you really think our son is ready to fill your boots? He is only twelve. You were thirty-one when you took over from your father."

"But I was prepared to take over much sooner than that!"

Emma put her arms around her husband's shoulders and gave him a big hug, "I remember your Mama telling me how you fretted and complained that you would never live long enough to take over from your old Pa."

Santa patted Emma's arms and laughed, "Ja, I was impatient. By Chris's age, I knew all there was to know about reindeer, and Pa boasted about my flying technique"

Frowning up at Emma, he asked, "Has he even spent three hours total time in the barn? Does he even know what a reindeer is?"

Emma sighed, sat across the table from him, and

poured herself a cup of cocoa.

"He spends all his time tinkering in the shop or doing I do not know what on that computer of his," Santa complained.

"He may be a little slow at handling reindeer, but he is a wiz in the toy shop. He is very like your Pa in that."

"Ja, Pa was a genuine toymaker. Ma used to say she had to shape his food into tin soldiers and rubber balls to get him to eat," Santa laughed.

Emma smiled as she always did at the sound of his deep, hearty ho, ho, ho.

"You were lucky. Pa knew his strengths. He was happy to retire early to spend more time making toys. Otherwise, you would have been fifty before you became Santa."

Santa shuddered then refilled his cup. He frowned as he sipped carefully at the hot liquid, "I cannot wait until Christopher is thirty-one or even thirteen. After a few hours of Christmas Eve deliveries, I can hardly walk! I can just see the headlines now, 'Santa found frozen in pain near Christmas tree'. Children all over the world will lie in their beds crying."

"They will worry about you."

"They will worry they will not get their presents."

"Now, Papa..."

"Well in any case, I have no choice. I have to retire, and Chris has to take up the reins in my place."

"If Chris takes over for you, he will be the youngest Santa ever. This is a big job for one so young," Emma took a slow sip from her mug.

Santa dropped his head into his hands and said, "He cannot even grow a beard. But I hate to disappoint all the children."

"Have you thought about Kristy taking your place?" said Emma.

"Kristy! She is only ten and a girl. Santa is a man. Santa has always been a man. I do not think people are ready for a woman Santa."

He saw Emma tighten her grip on her cocoa mug as she said, "I think you underestimate people, and your daughter."

"Chris is the only answer. He will be Santa, and he will begin in just a few short weeks," and with that Santa rose and stomped out of the room.

Chapter 3

Unlike Santa, when Kristy finished with the reindeer, she did not take the outside shortcut to the kitchen. Instead, like Chris, she took the longer route through the tunnel. She could not face 57 degrees below zero tonight.

As she approached the inside door, she called out, "I'm going to the library."

Eight more elvight dropped onto her head and shoulders.

"Now there are twelve of you!" Kristy did not mind. Like fire and light, they weighed next to nothing, and the lamps were not heavy either. The energy they gave off tickled Kristy wherever they touched her skin. When they entered the tunnel, Kristy's path filled with an elvight glow.

One elvight used Kristy's shirt to slide down her arm and settle on her cuff. In this position, Kristy studied the creature from the corner of her eye. Long and spindly, like a candle flame, it shone in streaks of purple and green like the Northern Lights. Kristy felt her shoulders and wrist warming from the heat they gave off.

"Wherever you are there is light and warmth," Kristy sang to the elvight. The nearness of elvight made her happy and when she was happy, she broke into song.

"I don't really know if you like my songs," she cooed. "You don't talk, you're so bright I can't see your faces, and you don't give off feelings like reindeer. But I'm not going to stop singing, so you are stuck with it."

By the time Kristy reached the library, only six elvight shone a soft light around her. The others had dropped off at shops along the way. Upon entering the room, two of the remaining elvight leapt to the large Picture Window. Kristy glanced at the window to check out the elvight's most recent work of art. Today the elvight finished a new picture made of light and the library window looked out on a green, tropical forest with a burst of bright flowers near enough and real enough to tempt Kristy to reach out and pick one. She had burnt herself before on them, so she knew better. Kristy gazed at the scene soaking up its light, warmth, and color. When the last elvight glided from her shoulders, she watched as they spread around the room. Two went off to join in a party happening in the fireplace, while the other four entered an elvight game that, to Kristy, seemed to consist of leaping and somersaulting aimlessly from candlestick to candlestick and back again.

Kristy scanned the room looking for her brother. The comfy sofa and chairs were all empty. She spotted him sitting at the big wooden desk. A leather-bound book lay open before him. Undisturbed by the elvight vaulting over his head, he had not looked up when she entered. He wore the hooded sweatshirt that matched the one she wore – his in blue, hers in green. Both read "N. Pole Coolest Place on Earth."

Looking at him, she supposed they did look a bit alike as people said. They both had jolly round faces like their father and straight dark hair like their mother. Chris's hair, cut short, never had a lock out of place. She reached up and tried to smooth down her long, messy hair. She only managed to snag a bit of moss clinging to it.

Next to Chris lay some of their favorite books: *Aerodynamics, Wind Velocity, Elf Magic, Do Reindeer Really Fly?* and *The Best Colors for Night Flying.* His nose was in the best one, *The Naughty or Nice Book.* Kristy moved to pace behind Christopher's chair.

"Come on, come on, Chris, just check all the 'nice' boxes after the children's names. I just finished feeding the reindeer for Dad and you. Dancer needed calming - you know how she gets when we're late with her moss. I'm tired and I want to go to bed."

Chris frowned at her from over the book, "I can't just mark nice after all the kids' names - some of them were naughty."

"Well, I know that," Kristy answered with an edge in her voice, "I've already marked the naughty ones."

Chris glanced down at the page before him then flipped forward one page, then two, and three, "Hey, some of these are marked! But how do you know?"

"Gosh Chris, get a grip. I keep a watch on the news all year long. It's the best use I've found yet for the web. I've had it with this last-minute stuff. The naughty reports come in from parents or teachers and I check the naughty box beside the little brat's name. Who has time to do it all in December?"

"But," Chris looked down and read, "Danny Wispgilly - Naughty. What did he do?"

"He took his sister's doll, the one she really wanted, the one that wets and poops."

Chris made a face.

Kristy shrugged, "I can't see it either, but hey, it's what she wanted, and she had been so good last year. She got it from Santa."

"So, he took her doll. Don't all brothers do that?"

Kristy sighed.

Again, you're not getting it. What a dunce. You might be great with toys. You might be inventive and great with the shop elves. As for people, you don't have a clue.

"Well," Kristy explained, slowly and with patience, "He didn't just take the doll away from his sister, make her scream, and then give it back. He's had the doll since February. The little brat has been holding it hostage threatening to decapitate it if his sister, Fiona, doesn't clean his room every week."

"Since February?"

"February."

"Does Fiona even know what decapitated means?"

"Of course not," Kristy answered rolling her eyes. "She doesn't even know what a dictionary is let alone how to read one. But like all sisters with evil brothers, she knows it's horrible."

"Does 'evil brothers' include me?"

Kristy looked away to keep him guessing. She let the silence stretch as she watched an elvlight dance on her fingertip.

"Since February," Kristy repeated drawing her attention back to her brother. "That is why 'naughty' is checked twice."

Chris glanced down, "So it is...."

"Rocks in his socks," Kristy recited.

"Seems only right," said Chris looking down at another name. "What about this Madeline Vincent? The naughty beside her name has been erased."

Without looking it up, Kristy said, "Reports in May said that Madeline wasn't doing her schoolwork and was disrupting class. A later report in September said that she had reformed. Now she's getting C grades, soon B's, and she has stopped picking on little Hugo Moreau."

Shaking his head Chris did as his sister said and finished the page in the *The Naughty or Nice Book* by marking all the 'nice' boxes. He left a pencil in the book to mark where he had left off. From under the book, Chris pulled out a familiar bit of paper with strange markings added. He sat back with a huge grin on his face.

"I want to show you what I did to Dad's itinerary. I tweaked his route for Christmas Eve, thereby saving him three hours over the course of the night," he said with pride.

"You really like working on this junk, don't you?" Kristy said looking over Chris's shoulder. "If I were you, I would spend more time learning how to fly reindeer and less time with your plans and inventions."

"Well, you're not me," Chris shouted as he slammed the map down on the desk. This was an argument they had before.

"Chris, I don't understand you. I dream of flying with Dad on Christmas Eve."

"So do I", Chris said slumping in his chair, "but I can't.

I can't fly."

"Of course not, you're not Peter Pan!"

Kristy sat on the desk and got right in her brother's face, "But you are the next Santa, Chris. Flying and delivering presents on Christmas Eve will be your job, and," she added with a sigh, "I wish that it would be mine."

"Well, when I'm Santa," said Chris as he sank even lower in his chair, "I'll have to call a delivery truck to take all those presents, because I can't do it."

Kristy pointed to *The Naughty or Nice Book* and shouted, "All those thousands of children do not want their presents delivered by someone in a brown suit driving a brown truck. They want someone jolly in a red suit driving a sleigh with eight tiny, *flying* reindeer." She just could not understand her brother, but it sure made her mad.

"I know what they expect, but it's not going to be me," said Chris turning red, "I'm afraid of heights."

First Kristy stared open-mouthed at her brother then doubled over. Loud, heavy laughs erupting from deep inside nearly knocked her onto her butt.

"I don't think it's a bit funny," said Chris crossing his arms over his chest.

Hearing tears in his voice, Kristy pulled herself together and stopped laughing. Kristy sensed that he regretted that he had let her in on his embarrassing secret.

"Sorry," she said, "you're right. It's not funny. I want to be Santa and you want to be Santa. Everything is all confused. What can we do about--"

Both children jumped as their father entered the room with a sad, worn look on his face. Kitchen smells of hot cocoa and baking entered with Santa. Three elvlight jumped from his shoulders to the Picture Window.

"Did you get *The Naughty or Nice Book* done?" Santa asked while he moved with a stiff walk toward the children. Kristy sat up straight sensing something serious about her father.

"We're almost finished Dad, we're at the V's" said Chris with only a slight waiver in his voice. "Is there a problem?"

"No, not a problem," Santa slowly answered, "not exactly."

Kristy looked at her brother, but he looked equally clueless. She waited to see if their father would let them in on what was troubling him.

He took a deep breath and said, "I am retiring after this year's Christmas Eve run. This will be my last year as Santa Claus." Santa sighed, "Christopher, you will be flying with me this year. It is time for you to become Santa."

Santa's words dropped like water balloons between Kristy and Chris and a damp chill filled the air. Chris looked at her. She could see his lower lip begin to tremble.

"Can I go too, Dad?" Kristy asked eagerly.

Santa glanced at his daughter and slowly, firmly shook his head, "You are too young."

All the color drained from Chris's face as he fell back into his chair.

"Dad, I'm not ready to be Santa," he pleaded. Kristy could tell Chris didn't want to confess the truth when he added, "I mean, I thought it would be years before I would be putting on the red suit."

Santa groaned when he knelt next to the chair. He

looked into Chris's eyes and said, "I cannot take this any longer. My back just cannot handle it. I need you. I know you can do this. It is in your blood. Think of all the Christmas cheer you will be passing out in just that one night."

Kristy said, "But Dad, he hasn't even finished school yet."

Ignoring this flimsy excuse, Santa moaned as he rose and headed for the door joined by half a dozen elvight. He looked back, gave Chris a wink, meant no doubt to reassure him, and said, "I know you can do this. You must." Then he pulled the door shut behind him.

Chris looked at her and said, "What am I going to do?"

"Don't worry," said Kristy sinking into the chair beside him, "We'll think of something."

Chapter 4

Morning found Emma in the warm, quiet kitchen. With her was the plump head of the house elves, Ginger. The aroma of fresh-baked bread had begun to radiate through the room from the huge, black stove in the corner by the time Kristy dragged herself in to join them. Emma brushed a fine dusting of flour off Ginger's hair as they stood at the table forming dough into loaves.

Kristy walked around the table to stand in front of one of the brightly painted cabinets. She took the doors in hand and fanned them back and forth in front of her face as she took great, slow breaths of air inhaling the scents of the spices packed inside. Cinnamon, cloves, spearmint and scores of others, Emma knew, made a heady mixture. Kristy took another deep breath before turning to her mother with a lazy, satisfied grin.

Emma looked up from the dough she had just placed in the next pan ready for the oven. She smiled warmly at Kristy. She knew her daughter's favorite thing to do in the kitchen was to smell all the spices at once. Pity she never wanted to do anything constructive with them.

"Are you ready for your baking lessons, Kristy?" She pointed to the thick, flour and grease spattered book next to her.

Kristy dragged herself next to her mother, pulled an apron over her head, and flipped a page of the book, but her eyes wandered to one of the windows with its view of falling snow. At that moment, Santa flew past the window. His sleigh was just visible under the Northern Lights.

"Mama, how did you learn to fly?"

"Fly?" Emma sighed as she caught the direction of her daughter's attention. "If I tell you will you buckle down and learn to make bread?"

It was Kristy's turn to sigh. A sigh Emma noticed was long, drawn out, and highly dramatic.

"Well, as you know," Emma began while she floured Kristy's hands and set her daughter to knead some dough, "after your father and I married, we moved in here with your grandparents. Grandma and Grandpa taught me all the Claus family traditions; the Santa duties – toy making, sleigh maintenance, feeding the reindeer, toy delivery; and the Mrs. Claus duties – caring for and milking the reindeer, overseeing the household chores, baking," Emma smiled softly at the memories. She saw herself in Kristy's place with globs of dough stuck to her fingers and her mother-in-law laughing good-heartedly because she had not known to flour her hands before touching the dough.

"One day I was flying with your grandfather to find a pregnant reindeer that had gotten lost. He noticed how I loved the feeling of freedom, that I was enjoying by being in the air. So it was then that he began my flying lessons."

"But Dad is a terrific flyer," Kristy said scratching her itchy nose on her shoulder. "Why didn't he teach you?"

"Good glory, Papa? Your father was just too busy. He said he could take me anywhere I needed to go. He actually thought housekeeping and reindeer tending would be enough to fill my days. Papa can be clueless sometimes."

"You love the reindeer, and I thought you liked to run the house?"

"Oh, I love the work. Caring for my home and family brings me such happiness."

"Glad someone likes it," Kristy grumbled.

"Now, Honey-cakes, we've been through this before. Until Christopher marries and there is a new Mrs. Claus, it will be your responsibility to assume my duties and care for the home and Santa. It's Claus family–"

"–tradition," Kristy finished. "Yeah, I know. But Mom, Dad loves being Santa and you love doing Mrs. Santa things. It works great for both of you. But for us..."

Kristy stopped as tears loomed in her eyes. In her head, Emma finished Kristy's sentences.

Chris likes the part of being Santa that involves toy making. I love the parts that Chris hates – feeding the reindeer and flying to deliver the toys.

As for the Mrs. Claus duties, Kristy dislikes them all. Chris is actually better in the kitchen, but only because he looks at cooking as chemistry experiments.

"Together the two of you would make one terrific Santa," Emma said thoughtfully, "but who would do my job?"

Kristy's face lit up impishly, "You've got lots of good years left in you, Mama. You won't have to retire for decades."

Emma laughed in spite herself. She watched Kristy's eyes turn toward the window again. Emma knew where her daughter's love lay. She didn't have the heart to force her to stay indoors practicing an art in which she had no interest. She gave Kristy a hug and a pat on the rear.

"Oh, good glory, go on," she said, "Go ahead to the barn."

Kristy carelessly wiped her hands on her apron, threw it to Ginger, and headed to the sink. She quickly rinsed her hands before pulling layers of clothing from the chest under the window. Emma continued to knead bread dough as she watched Kristy prepare for making the dangerous trip from house to barn. She smiled with approval but said not a word as her daughter climbed into green woolen pants and a jacket, then a pink fleece facemask and matching pink glove liners. Air-filled white rubber boots, a brown parka with a deep fur hood, and thick outer gloves completed the outfit. Kristy turned round to her mother and flapped one arm stiffly. Emma understood that Kristy was trying to throw her a kiss. She smiled at her very own gingerbread girl and threw her a kiss in return. Then she winced as the door slammed shut behind her.

Emma turned and looked down at Ginger. The red-haired house elf was dressed as usual in pristine white blouse and skirt. She topped that with a white, ruffled apron, which no amount of house cleaning ever managed to get dirty. Ginger always reminded Emma of a vanilla cupcake with strawberry frosting and a large cherry on top.

"Well," said Emma to Ginger who was furiously brushing flour and dough from Kristy's apron. "It looks like it's just us again."

"So much neater that way," Ginger answered in her crisp high-pitched voice. Emma just laughed her agreement.

Chapter 5

For the next whole week, Chris and Santa reviewed an endless list of all the things he needed to know about his new Christmas Eve position. They spent hours going over the Sleigh Checklist – a scroll so long that when unrolled it stretched from Chris's toes to his nose. Was the sleigh interior clean? Were the blades clean, sharp, and firmly connected? Behind the seat, the box that held the Santa Sack had to be free of any debris that would interfere with the gift magic. On, and on, and on it went until Chris was ready to barf.

Chris was tired of the poorly lit sled shed. The elvlight, huddled together in only two lamps, gave off light dimly and very little heat. Chris could tell this was not one of their favorite places either. The smell of leather and polar bear grease was beginning to get to him when Santa finally announced it was time to inspect the tack.

The tack room was part of the barn, so they set off through the tunnel to the barn. Though he was happy to be leaving the shed behind, Chris was not thrilled to be entering the barn. It smelled of dusty reindeer, their rather ripe food, and their always-stinky poop. How he longed to be in any of the toyshops with their smells of wood shaving, paint, and glue. He ached for the organized mess of his lab.

When Santa peered closely at him, Chris decided to pour on the charm and smile at his father as if he were in heaven on earth. To Chris, this seemed to reassure his father because he happily began to examine the tack, running bits of it gently through his hands as he commented on its condition in minute detail. Chris, bored out of his mukluks, tried not to yawn. His father had been telling him the same thing for years on end and he understood. The tack had to be in good condition: it could not be stiff or cracked. It just did not interest him.

He casually commented, "Dad, we could use nylon straps here. That would last longer, be stronger, and inspections would be shorter."

Santa stiffened, glared at him over his spectacles and said, "This equipment was good enough for my father, for my father's father, and his father. It's good enough for me."

Chris felt a weight settle on his chest and his lunch turned into a rock in his stomach. His distress must have shown on his face for his father's voice softened when he said, "But when you are Santa, you can do what you think best, I suppose."

One side of Chris's mouth rose in an attempt at a smile. He saw that his father meant well, even if he didn't quite get it.

Later, as they practiced hitching the reindeer into their traces, Chris spotted Kristy sneaking a peek at them from around the corner of the barn. Kristy haunted their every move. She seemed to be everywhere lately, watching everything he and Dad did. Like a sad and lonely ghost, she listened in on their conversations. She didn't smile and she never laughed when he made a mistake, and when it came to reindeer, he made many. He could see Kristy's mind working, easily absorbing those things which he found boring and that he struggled to learn but just couldn't quite grasp. She frowned at him now as he made a move to put Vixen in place behind Cupid. When she shook her head, he stopped and surveyed the reindeer he had already placed under his father's direction.

"No Vixen goes next to Prancer, not Donder," Chris muttered to himself. He peeked at Kristy as he moved Blitzen out of the Vixen spot, moved Vixen into it next to Prancer, and moved Blitzen to her spot next to Donder. He caught a glimpse of a lopsided smile as she ducked out of sight.

"See," Santa said, nodding at Chris's correction, "You are getting it!"

Chris grinned at his father. He appreciated the compliment, but in his heart, he knew it should be going to Kristy and not to him. Behind his smile a small voice was saying, "This will never work."

Chris struggled with the idea of revealing his terrible secret to his father. How could he tell his father, who was so full of misplaced hope in his son, that his son would not--could not ever take his place and become Santa? He knew his own limitations. Reindeer near him were nervous. Their eyes grew large as they watched for him to make a mistake that could hurt them. They shuddered at his touch and breathed a sigh of relief when he left them.

He preferred the solid walls of his nice warm toy shop, workrooms, and laboratory any day to wide-open spaces, snow, and blue skies. Especially not the sky - though it was lovely to look at. The clouds, from the ground, were soft and inviting. The distant stars at night lured him with their mystery, but he had no intention of getting any nearer, not if it meant he had to leave the ground, especially not in that sleigh: a non-airworthy vehicle designed for ground transportation.

Chris also knew where his talents lay. He could tinker for hours on the mechanics or circuitry of tools, household gadgets, and toys, especially toys. With his mother, he had devised a food processor run on elvight energy and elfin magic. He had made improvements to the sleigh that only Kristy knew about, but which someday he was sure his father would come to appreciate. In the toyshop, which was Santa's domain, Chris was careful to keep his improvements small so as not to draw unwanted attention from his father.

The laboratory, on the other hand, was all his. His father rarely visited him there, so in his lab, he gave free rein to all his creative urges. Hundreds of prototypes for every conceivable toy lay in boxes on shelves lining the room. Parts for dozens more were scattered over the lab tables. Chris smiled fondly at the thought of circuit boards, dolls' heads, and wiring lying in apparent tangles on one table, while unpainted wooden train parts and track cluttered another.

Chris quite simply did not want to be Santa.

A few days later, on her way to the barn, Kristy passed her brother trudging in the other direction. At least, she was almost sure it was Chris. He was covered head to toe with snow. The only thing that was showing was his red face that looked like it was ready to blow like a teapot on a hot stove.

In the barn, she found her father unhitching the reindeer from the sleigh. She started to help her father with his task, and she asked, "What happened to Frosty to make him so mad. Did he lose his corncob pipe?"

Santa peered over his spectacles at her, obviously not amused.

"If by 'Frosty' you mean your brother...I only wish I knew. We were going to work on his flying skills. Everything seemed fine at first, but when the sleigh got a foot off the snow, it jerked a little. I turned to see what had happened, and Chris dove headfirst out of the sleigh. He was rolling over the snow like tumbleweed in a hurricane. I turned the reindeer around to pick him up. He was as mad as a polar bear with a hot foot. He told me he likes to work on his flying by himself and stormed off."

Kristy bit her tongue. She didn't think it was her place to tell her father Chris's secret. She ran her hand down and around the smooth, bright cherry wood on the sleigh. Soon she was lost in dreams of soaring above the clouds on Christmas Eve, bringing bright smiles to small round faces. Her father's mumblings over things left unfinished, she tuned out as background noise. Thus, quite unaware of his growing frustration, she cut into his ranting.

"Dad, can we talk?"

Santa hung up the harness as the reindeer, steam puffing from their nostrils, trotted over to their food. Kristy thought he knew what was on her mind by his sigh and the look he gave her.

"Kristine, I know what you are going to say, but the job is unsuitable for you."

"Come on, Dad, I can do the same work as Chris. I am as strong, if not stronger, than Chris. Is it because I'm a girl or because I'm too young?"

Santa turned to Kristy and said, "You know how many years our family has been doing this job. In all that time, men have been Santa. You know kids see Santa as a jolly fat man with a beard and they are not the only ones. The world is not ready for a female Santa. It might be easier if you were not also a child."

Kristy cut in, "You just don't think I can do it."

Santa turned red with anger as if he were the one as mad as a polar bear with a hot foot. He steamed out of the barn and headed for the house as he yelled back to Kristy, "When you are done in there come in for supper."

"Yeah, I can finish doing your dirty work," Kristy muttered, "I can feed the reindeer. I can doctor the reindeer. I can hitch them to the sleigh. I can clean the sleigh. I can stock the barn and clean the barn. What part of this job is unsuitable for me?"

Chapter 6

One day, Chris was down at one of the workshops, with the noise of hammers pounding and saws ripping. Chris leaned over to explain the operation manual for his latest invention to Essen, a young shop elf who was so confused by this latest innovation, that he had begun to twist his mustache round his fine, nervous fingers. They stood before a truly remarkable, completely new machine.

Chris said, "Look here, it's basically a rectangular box with a hole at one end large enough for three of you to stand in shoulder to shoulder, and another hole at the other end of equal size."

Pointing at each element in turn, he continued, "At the front end is this large articulated arm with a claw waiting to pick up packages. At the far end is that large, padded basket on wheels. In between these large holes, you can see smaller arms waving about. They grab and feed lengths from those two dozen rolls of wrapping paper and ribbon suspended from the wires and tubes. The purpose of these gauges and peek holes dotting the surface and those levers..." A quick peek at Essen's empty look ended Chris's lesson, "...are maybe more than you need to know."

Essen smiled at that.

"It's really very simple," Chris said. "The Automatic, Self-Taping, Perfect Bow-Tying, and Present Wrapping Machine, or the ASWRAP for short will get the presents wrapped sixty-five percent faster than before. All you have to do is put gifts at this end and pick them up at the other end."

A barrel-shaped elf, so covered with white powdery flakes he looked a great deal like a snowball, interrupted the meeting. Chris recognized Essen's great sigh as one of relief as Essen ducked behind the ASWRAP with its 592-page manual.

"Christopher," said the second elf shouting over the noise of the shop, "Your father is looking for you. He needs to go over the proper way to handle the sleigh in too little or no snow."

Melting snow plopped off the snowball's head revealing Sam. Chris hung his head and said, "I will get there as soon as I finish here. Well, not right away. I must check the supplies in the paint shop, Sam."

Where Essen was a lean, angular elf of a nervous disposition, Sam was a mature elf of considerable girth and much patience. Chris could see by his frown that Sam was not pleased with the answer he had received. He knew Sam was very fond of him, but that he was also very loyal to his father.

Sam shook his head to dislodge more snow and asked, "Is there a problem Christopher? You seem to be avoiding your father. You are spending even more time working in the shops than usual."

When Chris did not answer, Sam said, "I hope you know you can talk to me about anything. I have been the head elf ever since your great grandfather, Chris Claus, became Santa."

Chris paced back and forth before he said, "How can you tell someone that you have a problem with something they need you to do, and you know you can't do it for them?"

"I do not think there is a problem so big that you cannot solve it by talking."

"Well, this is a big problem, Sam."

"You just need to talk to your father. He may get crazy mad at times, but he is there for you when you need him."

Chris doubted that was true in this case. Surprised, he asked, "Sam how did you know I was talking about Dad?"

"I may only be 374 years old, but I was not born yesterday," Sam huffed as he turned to go, splashing through the puddle he had made.

"Thanks Sam," Chris called after him. "Lunch everybody."

Chris watched as an articulated, metallic arm from the ASWRAP plucked Essen out of his corner and into the waiting jaws of the machine. As he passed the basket at the end of the ASWRAP, Chris patted the top of a beautifully wrapped but violently shaking package from which came muffled shouts.

"Don't worry Essen," he said laughing, "We'll have you out in time for Christmas."

But he was just kidding, and he stopped to unwrap the elf present. Leaving Essen to dust himself off, Chris walked down a hallway lined with old Claus family photos and portraits. An elvlight on his head and one on each shoulder joined Chris in his consideration of the groups of long-gone Clauses as he mulled over his troubles.

Here were Grandma and Grandpa Claus in a black and white photo waving from the sleigh as it flew over a lump of snow, which was the house.

"I hate flying."

A brownish photo showed Santa Chris Claus, his great-grandfather, posed with one of the Dashers.

"Reindeer make me itch."

He stopped before a photo of Kristy – her big old, fat red tongue hanging out as usual.

"She might take better pictures with pointy elf ears or maybe antlers."

"Mom looks great in pictures," he said as he paused before a photo of her in her youth. Her cheeks were full and rosy just as they were now and her brown eyes were gentle but sure.

Chris paused as a sudden grin broke out on his face. His eyes lit up into that lustrous black which indicated he had just come up with a brilliant idea.

"Why didn't you think of this before," he said smacking himself on the side of his head, "I know who I can talk to."

Chapter 7

Emma sat in the greenhouse jotting a note to herself.

Get Flora to trim the bushes. Prune the fruit trees next week. Check the vegetables for picking, also the herbs.

She inhaled the fragrances of rich, fertile soil and the perfume of dozens of flowers growing in beds scattered throughout the garden. Looking around, she smiled with pleasure at all the shades of green and the ruby, sapphire, and golden hues of rare and fragrant flowers. Hundreds of elvight in light colors of white and gold - Emma had found them the best colors for growing plants - in the dome above made it as bright as noon on an Iowa lake. It brought her memories of cornfields in August.

Emma sat in her special corner at a small writing desk. Around her, yellow roses grew thick on bushes and climbed up heavily laden trellises. Pink roses and red ones grew side by side in planters and pots.

Kris might call this spot "of no obvious use," but I find him napping on the grass here often enough.

Notepad before her and pen in hand, Emma put on her sunglasses and stared at elvight dancing all around her and in and about the flowers.

"I think this is your favorite spot at the North Pole too," she said to them.

No response as usual. It is not that I love gardening so much. I would rather spend my time cooking or baking.

A field elf walked by, trowel in hand. To him she said, "I supposed you miss Connie Claus. She had a green thumb. She hated any day when she had no time to dig in the dirt. Sorry I leave so much work for you."

"It is truly our pleasure, Ma'am," he said and tipped his cap to her.

No, I love the rose garden because here I do not have to work hard. It is so soothing to watch the elvight flitting about, swinging from branch to branch, and humming. I guess studying them is my own special hobby. I can sit back and relax because I am rarely disturbed.

"Mom!" Chris said, coming up behind her.

Emma jerked and threw her pen across the desk. It landed some five feet away, stuck in the dirt and quivered there.

"Good glory, Christopher, you should not sneak up on a person like that!"

"Sorry, Mom," Chris said lowering his head. "I didn't mean to scare you."

"I wasn't scared, dear," removing her sunglasses, Emma replied, "You just startled me was all."

Emma looked at her obviously dejected son and pulled him over to sit on the desk close to her side, "What's the matter, pumpkin?"

"Oh, Mom," Chris weakly protested and then blushed.

"What is it?" Emma coaxed as she squeezed Chris's chin.

"Everything."

"Oh, now, what can be that bad?"

"Me being Santa."

"Oh, yes," she agreed, "that would be bad."

"What?"

"Just go ahead with what you were saying, dear."

Chris frowned at her then continued as she had asked, "I cannot be Santa. I can't fly." He took a deep breath and finally the words just exploded out of him, "I'm scared of heights!"

"Yes, I know dear."

"You know?"

"Well, I suspected as much."

"How?"

"Mothers know these things dear." Emma stood and gave her son a good, solid squeeze, "from the time you were quite small I noticed that you seldom left the ground. When Kristy was risking life and limb to climb the cupboards in search of treats, you were waiting below for her to toss them down."

Chris's face was blank. Emma realized that he had no memory of that. She hunted her memory for another example. Soon her face lit up and she said, "You were fine on the reindeer as they walked in the paddock or around the barn, but the minute they bunched their muscles to take flight you slipped off their backs like they were greased pigs."

"But, Mom, if you know, why does Dad still think I can be Santa?"

"Because your father does not know."

Chris stared open mouthed at her, "You know, but you didn't tell him?"

"Suspected," Emma corrected. "Over the years I have pointed some things out to him. Like the way you always let Kristy do the climbing."

"Right, in the barn I always make Kristy climb into the hayloft for the feed."

"And you wait below just like you did for the cookies. Your father decided you were cautious."

"Cautious?"

"Yes, and he thinks you've grown out of it."

"But I haven't, Mom," Chris groaned, "it's only gotten worse."

"I am truly sorry to hear that, dear."

When Chris's lower lip began to tremble, Emma took him in her arms again and held him tight.

In a sad, shaky voice Chris said, "Are you disappointed in me?"

"Disappointed?" Emma said with a tiny chuckle, "Why, no pumpkin. You are the way God made you. We all have our little quirks."

"Quirks," Chris said in a voice so loud his mother cringed and backed away. "Quirks--this is more than a quirk, Mom! This is serious. My little quirk could be the end of eons of Claus family tradition..."

"Eons, dear, is a bit of an exaggeration."

"Mom, the point is that Dad expects me to take over for him and I can't do it."

"That's true, dear, you can't."

Chris let out a tight scream, squeezed his hands into fists, and pounded the desktop, scattering nearby elvight to hide in the foliage. "I will ruin everything! Those children will not receive presents – I can't bear it! How do you think that will make Dad feel? I am a failure."

"You are not a failure," Emma sternly replied shaking her finger at him. "You are creative and inventive and will probably be the finest Master Toymaker of all time. You have not let down the family or the family tradition. Santa Claus, by tradition is also a Toymaker."

"But more importantly, once a year Santa Claus pulls on his red suit, hitches eight tiny reindeer to his sleigh, and *flies* all around the world delivering presents." Again, Chris screamed as he slammed his fist on the desk scattering the few elvight who had been brave enough to return, "And I cannot fly!"

"That's okay, dear," Emma soothed as she patted him on the back. "You still haven't let the family down. We still have Kristy."

Chris's hands relaxed as he sagged down to lie on the desk. He let out a long, exasperated sigh and said, "But Dad will not hand his job over to a little girl."

"I know that too, dear."

"Mom!"

"I do know your father pretty well after all, and if there's one thing I'm sure of it's that his mind is set in stone on that point."

"You're not being much help, Mom. Can't you talk to him?"

"Dear," Emma said as she began to pace in the tight space around the desk, "there are some things your father just does not want to hear from me."

"Well, I can't tell him," Chris said.

"No, I'm pretty sure he wouldn't believe it if you tried. It would just be a waste of breath."

"Not to mention he gets darn mad."

"Well, dear, that may be because of all the pain he's in."

"His back?"

"Yes, being Santa Claus is hard on his back. All that lifting, stooping... Not to mention the sleigh ride in the cold night air and all those chimneys to leap down."

Chris shuddered at those last words.

"Sorry, dear," Emma said when she saw that Chris had gone a little pale. "I guess you do have it bad."

"But Mom, what can we do?"

Emma resumed her seat. When she moved to set her elbows on the desk, Chris sat up to make room for her. She rested for a moment with her head in her hands and this time she really did stare off into space. After a while, she shook her head and looked up at Chris.

"We cannot simply tell him. Your father is not the sort swayed by words. He will only believe what he sees for himself with his own eyes. So, we will have to show him."

Chapter 8

Two days before Christmas Eve, Chris was ready to reveal his plan to Kristy. He knew he had to do it in a way that she would appreciate. His sister was a drama queen as far as he was concerned, so it had to be unveiled theatrically. Knowing that Kristy had finished in the barn for the day, Chris didn't bother to look for her there or in any adjoining storerooms. If she had been in any of the toy labs or workrooms, he would have known, so he sneaked through the house room by room looking for her.

In the kitchen--the last room where he expected her to be and so the first room he tried, his mother just laughed when he asked if Kristy had been there recently. His father, alone in his study poring over flight plans, told him to try the library. In the library, a dozen elvight twittered sharply when he disturbed them at the Christmas Picture Window. They were busy preparing for its annual unveiling on Christmas morning. Kristy was not there.

He checked his own room, just in case. The brown and beige plaid comforter was taut and unwrinkled. Neither the computer nor the papers on his desk were disturbed.

The remote-controlled planes attached to the ceiling did not sway. Nothing was out of place and there were no messes - Kristy had obviously not been here.

Chris risked a quick peek into Kristy's bedroom by opening the door just a crack. Kristy's room was a curious mix of colors. It had once been pink – a color Kristy could no longer tolerate. Instead of repainting, she did her utmost to disguise it. Around the walls, Kristy had hung shelves for books and stuffed reindeer. Posters of the latest musical stars had been plastered in no particular order on the walls between the shelves, along with Kristy's own sketches and paintings of reindeer and elves. It looked normal - bed unmade, clothes strewn all over. Just because Chris couldn't see her didn't mean Kristy wasn't buried in there somewhere under all that junk, but it was much too quiet for her to be in here.

The last room he searched was the living room. He approached it on tiptoe and opened the door slowly, squeezing through just before it reached the squeaking point. Dean Martin's Christmas music--Kristy's favorite--floated over to meet him. He scanned the room slowly. It was difficult to see. The only light came from a few elvight in the fireplace. No one sat at the game table or at the snack bar nearby. The conversation pit was dark and empty. Chris suspected that Kristy was on the sofa in front of the elvight fire. It was a very large sofa, high backed and over-stuffed, easy to get lost in.

Chris crept past the family Christmas tree, frosted with elfin 'no-melt snow', with its gold balls and white lights and tinsel made of elvight strands. Peering over the back of the couch, he could see that Kristy was in one of her 'Do Not Disturb' modes. Bundled up in her ratty, old bathrobe – the quilted one with the batting poking out, her face was set in a rock-solid frown.

"I know what we're going to do," Chris shouted in his best 'ta-da' voice.

Kristy screamed, jumped up, and socked him in the shoulder.

"Ouch!" He cried.

"Serves you right," Kristy said, "sneaking up on me like that. That's a nasty habit you really must break."

Chris rubbed his shoulder and tried again, "Sorry, but I really do know what we're going to do about Christmas Eve."

"What do you mean 'we'?" Kristy snapped. "You're the one who is supposed to be spreading Christmas cheer all over the land. Not me - I'm just a baby!"

"The baby part may be true..."

Kristy made a fist.

"Aw, now don't be like that, Kristy. I'm giving you your Christmas gift early," Chris grinned as he pulled out a red, fur trimmed hat and plunked it down on her head. This time he actually did say, "Ta-da!"

"My gift to you is that you are now Santa."

Kristy's eyes crossed as she stared at the fuzzy, white ball hanging between her eyes, but she didn't crack the slightest smile, "I think this is a pretty cruel joke."

"It's no joke. I'm serious!"

"You can't do this," Kristy said as she flopped back down onto the couch. "Only Dad can pass on the Santa suit."

"Almost right," he replied, "only *Santa* can pass this on." He plopped down close to Kristy so she had to look at him. She gave him one of her sourest looks. He thought it made her look meaner and uglier than usual.

Chris, wishing that just for once his sister could be less cranky and more cooperative, swallowed a lump as dry as a cotton ball before he continued, "Just today Dad passed it down to me. He didn't make a big show of it. We were in the sleigh testing the seat padding. Just when I thought I might be bored into a permanent state of petrification, he pulled this hat out of his pocket, flourished it around for a moment, then plopped it on my head.

"Son," Chris said lowering his voice. His imitation of their father brought half a smile to Kristy's face. "Son, in just two short days you will be making your Christmas Eve training flight and I will be making my last Christmas Eve flight. The formal passing will be made during the Christmas party, after we return from my last ride. I am giving this to you now as a symbol of my intention to pass the Santa Suit on to you. I know it will fill you with a sense of the honor that the position bestows, and also that it will give you the strength to overcome any last reservations you may have.'"

Kristy stared at him with fire in her eyes, "What did you say?"

"Not much," Chris slumped deeper into the couch.

Kristy sniffed and rubbed her sleeve under her nose.

"I thanked him, of course, but I'm not sure I sounded thankful."

Chris jumped up and grinned right into Kristy's face, "But you're missing the point. He passed me the hat – temporarily to be sure, but pass it he did. For a short while, that makes me Santa. Now, I'm passing it on to you. I'm giving the hat to you because you are the one who is right for this job. Not me, I would pass out when the reindeer got ten feet off the ground. You can fly rings around me and probably Dad."

Kristy squeezed her brother's cheeks, but anger still simmered in her eyes, "Reindeer poop...."

Chris winced and wagged a finger at his sister, "Language, Kristine, language."

"Okay, but no more kissing up to me," Kristy smirked and poked her own finger into his stomach as she mocked him, "but Dad still will not allow this, because I'm a little girl."

Chris sensed his sister's resentment, and he shared in her frustration, but his grin only got wider as he rubbed his stomach and replied, "I have a plan that will show Dad who should be Santa in his place and if it doesn't convince him, it will make you Santa for at least this one Christmas Eve."

Chapter 9

Finally, it was Christmas Eve, and the North Pole was like a beehive, everyone buzzing around with frantic last-minute preparations. Santa watched from the kitchen window. He felt the tension in the air, for this year was to be his last flight and the new Santa's first.

Out of his sight, Santa knew that one crew of elves wrapped last minute presents and another bunch hustled them to the Elfin Prep Cell. There each gift was sprinkled with magic and shrunk to fit into the Santa Sack. He watched as the Santa Sack emerged from the EPC wearing a red, green, and white halo. The elves tossed it into the back of the sleigh.

Emma was putting the final touches on Santa.

"Now Papa, do you have your itinerary? Are you wearing your long johns? You know it is cold out there."

"Yes, yes, Mama," answered Santa. As Emma spun him around to fuss with his buttons, Ginger flew past with a dustpan in her hand. He felt a short blast of cold air as the door quickly opened and closed behind him. "I don't see the children, yet. I hope Chris won't be late."

Santa braced his back to lessen the pain when he reached for his hat on a table next to them.

"Your back again, Kris?"

"Ja, Mama, I sure am glad Chris will be with me. I don't think I can do much tonight."

Handing him his gloves, she said, "Don't worry about your son. I spoke with him earlier. He knows what time he is to meet you at the sleigh."

Santa tucked in his scarf and headed to the door. Outside, waited the freshly repainted sleigh and eight reindeer, surrounded by elves busily double-checking the tack. In the front seat, huddled a small figure clothed in a red, woolen over-jacket much like his own. The fur-lined hood of the Inuit parka, under the woolen coat, completely enclosed Chris's head. Santa smiled in satisfaction; the fur parka would protect his son's face until his beard grew in.

As Santa approached, the elves burst into, "Here Comes Santa Claus"! He joined them in laughing at their yearly joke, happy he would never have to hear it again.

A cold breeze bit Santa's cheek as he climbed into the sleigh, but he knew that this job that warmed his heart would thaw his face throughout the chilly night. As he settled into the seat, a loud fart sound erupted from the cushions. Holly and Molly, the twin elves standing next to the sleigh, gave each other high fives. This was their favorite joke. They played it every year. Santa ignored the twins but he turned to his trainee and laughed, "Well, Chris, this is a night you will never fart-get!" He laughed so hard he shook like a bowl of jelly.

Santa received a 'thumbs up' from a mittened finger, so he continued more seriously, "When you leave a present for the children, they also give you a gift. You get a little piece of love and joy from each child. It will stay with you all year long."

Santa took the reins in his hands, "I'll let you handle the take-off from another place. I want to do it one last time from here."

When he looked over the elves one last time, he found them swimming through the tears in his eyes, then he faced forward and called, "Now, Dasher! Now, Dancer! On, Prancer... Oh, you know what comes next. Let's go!"

The sleigh hurtled through the falling snow. Santa listened without a word to the elves fading song.

"I'll find a smooth area of pack ice for you to try a take-off and landing by yourself," Santa said. He tried to break the silence which had grown as stiff as wet mittens in a polar wind. He wanted to test Chris's handling of the sleigh in the cold and blowing snow.

Santa's beard filled with snow as they flew through the cold, still night.

"I know a great place you can take off from. There is a frozen lake nestled in a valley on the New Siberia Islands. Smooth for miles, it will be perfect."

With a snap of the reins, the sleigh picked up speed flying low over the cold sea. Now as the night cleared, the pack ice looked like sand in a desert upon which someone had sprinkled sugar crystals. As they approached the islands, the ice began to change, and he could see how the shifting ice flows had heaved upon the rocks and shoreline, as if a small mountain range of ice were escaping from the sea.

With a slight smirk on his face, Santa glanced over at

his hooded passenger thinking now would be a good time to show his son his skill with the reindeer. He dropped the sleigh much lower and hurtled left around a large boulder. The runner on the sleigh struck snow, kicking it into the air. He twisted to the right around some jagged, razor-sharp ice, making the sleigh dance over large chunks of snow-covered boulders.

Now the big island was ahead of them. A fifty-foot wall of rock rose out of the sea to greet them. Santa laughed and flew straight up the bluff. The reindeer used their hoofs to push off the edge, propelling the sleigh up and over the top. A familiar 'oomph' in his stomach made Santa laugh aloud.

"I hope I didn't scare you too much," Santa shouted over the roar of the wind.

Chris is taking this well. Just a week back he would have jumped out long ago. He must have found his sky legs.

They headed toward the mountains on the far side of the island. The bright moon highlighted the snow blown waves on the tundra below. Santa slowed to let his son see the wild reindeer now running beneath them. They ran to keep up with the sleigh. Once in a while, an individual would leap out of the snow cloud being kicked up by the herd. One arched his necked and looked up at them as if to say, I want to fly with you.

On a frozen lake at the foot of a small mountain on the southernmost island, Santa landed the sleigh. He stepped out onto the ice, handed the reins to his son, and said, "Now it's your turn son. Let's see what you've got."

Before he could take a breath, the sleigh shot off into

the night. Santa's jaw dropped as he watched his son and the reindeer performing aerial magic with the colorful northern lights providing an enchanting backdrop. The sleigh twisted, turned, and danced in loops and figure eights, then blasted off to the top of the mountain where its blades tapped the snowy rise before zooming back down the slopes like a downhill ski racer.

Standing on the ice Santa puffed up with pride. He had never seen such a natural union between reindeer and driver.

A seamless performance. I knew he had it in him.

Suddenly Santa heard a boom beneath his feet followed by a sound like cracking glass.

"I think I need to lose some weight," Santa muttered as slowly he began to sink.

As the icy water rose to his ankles, the sleigh returned, and a hand pulled Santa up to the runner. With relief and gratitude, Santa dragged his body onto the runner, but terror replaced gratitude as the all too familiar sharp and burning pain shot across his lower back and down both his legs.

How will I get back in the sleigh?

A shaky and surprisingly tiny voice asked, "Are you all right, Dad?"

Santa drew on all his strength of will to pull himself into the seat. After a few deep breaths, the pain subsided. Santa looked down at his soggy boots then his head snapped up to stare at the sleigh's driver. Sure enough, there, peering out of the fur-lined hood, were the light-brown eyes of his daughter and not the dark ones of his son.

"All right, young lady, what are you doing here?" barked Santa, "and where is your brother?"

Kristy did not have time to answer. She flew the sled to firm ground in the hills above the lake. With the reindeer firmly settled, she jumped from the sleigh and approached Donder.

"Can I borrow your feed bag?"

Donder nodded and Kristy removed the feedbag and ran to a snowdrift. She filled the bag with fresh, cold snow and brought it back to the sleigh. Pulling her father forward, she gently placed the ice pack on his lower back, pushed him upright, and then jumped back into the sleigh.

"Now see here," Santa sputtered, insulted by Kristy's offhand treatment yet impressed by her quick thinking. *So much like her mother!*

"Wait, Dad," said Kristy. She reached across his lap to open a panel in the dashboard. Out popped a cup holder with two mugs of steaming hot cocoa.

Kristy handed him a mug, "Don't question it, Dad. Just drink it up. We need to get you warm. I'll leave Chris's heater open to keep you from freezing."

"Heater," repeated Santa. He was amazed, but very grateful. The heater and the cocoa spread their warmth to his chilly feet.

Kristy climbed back in the sleigh, snapped the reins, and made a clicking noise in her cheek. The reindeers' ears perked up and, as a team, they vaulted into the sky. Now Kristy had time for explanations.

"This was Chris's idea. You see," she continued quickly, "he wanted to give me the chance to be Santa at least this one night, and he didn't want to disappoint you and all the children."

"Okay," Santa's voice had a hard edge as he replied, "this little joke is over. Turn the sleigh around."

He watched the tears form in Kristy's eyes and promptly freeze as they slid down her cheeks.

"But, Dad, we'll lose so much time and, Dad, I've dreamed of this night for years. You don't know how I feel. I see my father spread all this love and joy over the world each year, and what do I get to do? I sit at home and dream about the day that I can do it too. Like you said, Dad, it's in our blood, but I'll never get to be Santa because I'm a little girl and the world and you aren't ready for that."

Santa felt the pain throbbing in his lower back, and he was certain he would not be able to do much climbing around tonight. He also knew turning the sleigh around was no longer an option, as time was running against them.

"You're right about the world," Santa said, "but I have a job to do and no time now to correct your and Christopher's mistakes. I will have to settle for your help this year. At least it will give your brother a whole year to work on his flying skills."

Santa pulled the reins from Kristy's hands and resumed their flight itinerary. Next to him, Kristy sighed.

"Where on earth did you learn to fly like that?" Santa asked. He was in awe of her talent and quick wits under pressure, but he would not admit it.

"Mostly by watching you work with Chris, some from Mom. She takes me up now and then."

"Your mother!" replied Santa, "I didn't know your mother liked to fly."

"Really, Dad," Kristy said, "She loves it too and she's good at it."

They flew in silence until Santa could see the lights of the first house on their schedule.

He pointed down and to their left, "Look, Kristy, it was my first house--the first time I flew with my Papa."

Kristy smiled and bounced a little in her seat. Her excitement thawed him a bit, despite himself.

Without a sound and without a bump, Santa settled the sleigh on the first roof. He reached in the back to pull out the red bag that was stowed there. And that's when the second spasm hit. He gasped as the pain renewed in sharp stabs up his back and down his legs.

"Dad, are you all right?"

"No, Kristine, I am not," Santa managed to say. "Can you reach the Santa Sack?"

"Sure," she said and stood on the seat to retrieve the big, red bag.

"You are going to have to help me with this Kristine."

Kristy's face shone.

"You know how the magic Santa Sack works?"

Kristy nodded, "I've studied your work. I know what to do."

Studied my work?

She opened the sack and oohed in delight. Tiny presents, lifted by magical light, grew as they rose to the top.

"It's wonderful," she said.

As she left the sleigh, Kristy recited one of the lessons she had overheard, "I first take a deep breath, then let it out slowly. That will not only make me slimmer, it will slow me as I drop. When I want to come back up the chimney, I again take a deep breath. This breath I also release slowly using my breath as a sort of jet propulsion to push me back up to the roof."

Amazing, she is quoting me word for word. Kristy is as fascinated by my profession as I was by my father. I have not seen that in Christopher.

Kristy slipped over the edge of the chimney. At first, she dropped like a rock and her stomach jumped into her throat. Before she hit the bottom, she slowed, as she knew she would, and she floated to a stop. Santa slid down the chimney behind her. Together they tiptoed across the pine-scented room to the Christmas tree. Reaching into the Santa Sack, Santa pulled out a gift for a girl named Sarah - a wriggling puppy with a green ribbon attached to his collar. Next out came a present for Matthew – an electric train set. One wrapped present for each of them, he slid under the tree. After watching Santa at the tree, Kristy approached the mantel where she filled the stockings with small toys, fruit, and nuts. She turned to see her father struggling to get up from his knees. She ran over to help him.

Santa gave her a grateful smile, "Thank you for your help. I really am unable to do the work tonight. I am afraid you will have to help a lot."

They heard a happy yip from the puppy at their feet. Kristy looked down to catch the puppy finishing the soft, sweet cookie that had fallen from the table when Santa used it as a brace to get up. With the disappearance of the last crumb, Santa looked as though he had missed his last meal.

As soon as she stepped into the fireplace and exhaled a deep breath, Kristy flew up the chimney like soda pop sucked up a straw. Santa followed Kristy up the chimney, then she helped him into the sleigh.

Santa handed the reins to her, "Well, I know you can handle this part of the trip," he said and leaned back in the seat with his hands behind his head.

In the blink of an eye, a beaming Kristy had the reindeer off the roof and, keeping to the itinerary, they visited the rest of the homes in that village. They finished in good time and flew away. Behind them, Kristy glanced at candles gently lighting some of the shrinking windows.

They are winking us goodbye.

Chapter 10

The light of the moon brightened the snow-blanketed yard and created a sparkling path to the farmhouse of Kristy's next stop. She brought the sleigh softly down on the roof over the head of another sleeping child.

Santa put out his arm to stop her, "This home has given me a lot of problems the last few years."

Kristy looked at him closely.

What is he up to?

When he didn't add any more, she snatched the Santa Sack and swooped down the chimney. At the bottom, she peeked around the bricks of the fireplace and carefully scanned the room. It was dark, lit only by the flickering lights of a Christmas tree in the far corner. Still, Kristy saw nothing that could cause a problem. The long stretch of hardwood floor from here to the tree was bare. Put on edge by her father's words, she tiptoed lightly across the room. As she slid a gift under the tree, a deep growl, like the sound of an angry buzz saw, started up so close behind her that she could feel the vibration on the seat of her pants.

Kristy popped up to the roof with a huge grin on her face.

"How did you get out of there?" Santa asked, "I didn't even hear a bark from that vicious dog."

"I just did what I've done at every house that has a dog," Kristy answered, "I fed him the milk and cookies."

"Oh... I never thought of that. So you don't eat the cookies first thing?"

"First thing? No, I do it last, if at all. I've been full since the third stop that left cookies anyway. I've just been taking a nibble out of each cookie," Kristy paused, a look of concern growing over her face. "Was that wrong? Is there a Santa Rule that says Santa must eat all the cookies, right away, first thing?"

"Oh, no, not that I'm aware of," Santa assured her, "it's just where I naturally go first is all. That was very smart of you. If I had thought of that, I might not be so round and jolly now and I would have figured out the dog problem long ago. I guess I just love the milk and cookies too much. Speaking of which--"

"Yes, Dad," Kristy cut in, "next stop I'll bring you the cookies. Unless, of course, there's another mean dog."

They join in loud ho, ho, hos as Kristy snapped the reins to start the reindeer toward their next stop.

"We are nearly out of Russia now," Santa said.

"Out of Russia?" Kristy said. "But we hardly made any stops."

"That is because most Russians do not believe in Santa Claus. They receive gifts from Baboushka on the fifth of January."

"Does that happen a lot? Do we have other bare spots?"

"Certainly, in Asia for example, there are not many believers. Thus, we do not have many stops. Our heaviest work is over North America."

Her "oh" turned into, "oh no" when Comet's tail started twitching.

"You know what that means," Santa said.

Kristy moaned. She did know.

It's never good for reindeer to poop in the air. It might end up on you!

She landed in a valley to give Comet a chance to relieve herself.

Several minutes later, they were back in the air and Blitzen's tail started twitching.

"Is this usual, Dad?"

"Bad luck, now you'll have to land again."

Down they went again so Blitzen could do her duty. Several minutes later, they were back in the air and Cupid's tail started twitching.

"They must be sick," Kristy cried in alarm. "What do we do?"

"For a start, I would land," said Santa.

Kristy worried seriously about the reindeer's health. After she landed, she checked Comet, Blitzen, and Cupid's pulses and felt their stomachs. Kristy was puzzled. She could sense no distress coming from the reindeer, so she looked in Cupid's eye. Not only did she find no discomfort, there actually was a sparkle in Cupid's eye and she knew what that meant.

The reindeer began to make jolly, happy clicking nois-es and suddenly her father, Kristy saw, was about to bust a gut laughing.

"A joke," Kristy yelled, "This was all a joke!"

"It's those elves," Santa stopped rolling around the seat long enough to reply, "This time with a little coach-ing from your mother. They did it to me twice before I caught on."

Santa resumed his laughter as Kristy climbed back into the sleigh and snapped the reins.

"We'll have no more of that," she ordered in a voice that, even to her, sounded like her mother. The reindeer calmed down and leaped obediently into the air.

After Santa got his breath back, he explained to Kristy, "The elves are great workers in the house, shops, and out-doors, and they have very creative and intelligent minds. Also, between those pointy ears is a wonderful sense of humor or so they think. Christopher had better be pre-pared when he takes over, because in some of them it comes out in practical jokes like that one.

"One time", Santa chuckled, "I remember walking into my peaceful office. Elvight were leaping from the Picture Window to my desk, making it look like warm, summer sunlight was streaming through the window at an angle. They lit up my desk, upon which sat a colorful, metal box. Next to the box lay a handwritten letter. As I moved around my desk to sit in the chair, I reached over to grab my reading glasses. As I slipped them on, I noticed that the cube-shaped box in front of me was some form of Jack-in-the-Box.

"I remember elvight tickling my head as they played

on the back of the chair. I picked up the letter and unrolled it to read, 'Dear Santa, here is a new Jack-in-the-Box for your inspection. Hope you like it! If you do, we will immediately start mass-production for next Christmas.' It was signed by Essen on behalf of the shop Elves.

"I set the letter down and picked up the metal box. Because of the elvlight, it was warm to the touch. The cube was beautifully painted on all sides, on the top and even on the bottom. On the front, Humpty Dumpty was teetering on the wall. I turned it to the right and there sat Little Jack Horner in his corner. When I turned it again, Little Miss Muffin was having a light lunch. Turning it once again revealed Jack and Jill skipping hand in hand up the hill. On the bottom, a monkey was chasing a weasel around a cobbler's bench.

"I leaned back in my chair and put my feet up on the desk to get comfortable. The top of the Jack-in-the-Box pictured four and twenty black birds sitting around the edge of a pie. The top crust of the pie was the hinged lid where Jack should spring from at the end of the tune. I was fascinated by the box and how much effort had gone into its creation. I grabbed the red wooden knob on the crank and started to turn it. A delightful little tune came out of the box with the winding of the knob. I sang along with the tune, '...the monkey chased the weasel...'

"The box looked so wonderful I was anxiously waiting to see what the marvelous 'Jack' would be like. Turning the handle faster in anticipation, I shouted the word 'pop' out loud. Suddenly, my glasses were covered with a white and yellow blur. I licked my lips and discovered the taste of a delicious banana cream pie. I removed my glasses, wiped my face clean, and finished eating what was left of the pie that had struck me square in the face.

"Setting the Jack-in-the-Box down, I laughed as I saw a small pie tin on the end of a spring where the puppet should have been. Those crazy elves had gotten me again!"

Kristy felt better now and joined her father in his laughter.

"And one time - this was early in my career - the elves told me that the Johnson house in Bemidji had installed a new fireplace and chimney during the year past. They said it was a large thing. I hardly needed to suck my gut in. They like to kid me about my weight. Anyway, when I arrived it was as they had described - a large handsome chimney of clean, red bricks. There was no smoke coming from the lip. Reassured by its black darkness, I grabbed my bag, took a leap, and landed with a bone-shaking thud on the roof with chimney up to my thighs. When the roof stopped vibrating and my knees stopped shaking, I climbed out of the artificial chimney and listened for any uproar from inside the house. I was mighty relieved that the thunderous shock I had just made on the Johnson's roof had not awakened the whole neighborhood! I swear you could hear those elves laughing all the way from the North Pole."

Santa had to grab the reins while Kristy rolled into a ball laughing.

On the way to the next town, Santa leaned over to whisper in Kristy's ear, "Okay, little girl, how did you get up and down those chimneys so fast?"

Kristy took a long look at her father's belly before she replied, "Come on, Dad, it's easy, I'm not as big as you. Plus, I don't know how you can even fit into some of those chimneys."

They both laughed as she swooped down to land on the ground beside the next house, which had no chimney. Before Kristy could grab the sack, Santa pushed her down so that her head was below the sled's rim.

"Keep quiet," he whispered.

Suddenly he froze stiff, then his head turned in short, quick movements, and his hands began to jerk up and down.

Holy reindeer poop! What's wrong with my Papa, Kristy wanted to shout. Instead, she crammed her mittens into her mouth, biting her fingers.

Then Santa stopped jerking, relaxed, and patted the seat beside him, inviting Kristy to come back up. Santa must have seen the shock on her face because he nearly choked on his hearty ho, ho, ho, "Don't worry, daughter, I'm not having a fit. I learned a trick a while back. Just as we landed, a man peered out that window across the street. Now he thinks his neighbors have one outstanding Christmas display in their front yard."

Kristy joined in her father's glee. Her ho, ho ho a soprano counterpoint to Santa's deep, bass laugh. When their chuckling subsided, she readied herself to get on with the job at hand. She smiled up at her father with a sly grin, "Now I get to find out how you get into houses without fireplaces. Chris and I tried to figure that one out but couldn't and Mom would not tell us."

Chuckling, Santa reached under the seat and pulled open a secret drawer. He grabbed something shiny and hid it in his mitten-covered fist. Kristy held out her hands and he let the object drop into them. She peered at it in the uncertain light. It was a key of some kind.

"It's a skeleton key," Santa explained, "a little bit of elfin magic."

Kristy looked again. Yes, it was – a key in the shape of a skeleton. But she still was not sure.

"Go ahead. Give it a try," he said and his deep ho, ho, ho followed her to the door.

At the door, Kristy shook the key, making its bones jangle and ring on the chain. She didn't see how this sloppy, old key was going to open anything. But she knew that Christmas Eve was a magical night, a night for belief. She brought the key up close to the lock and watched in amazement as it first glowed red. Then the key skull peered into the lock, rearranged its bones, turned green, and jumped into the keyhole. The door swung open, and the skeleton key popped back out and into Kristy's waiting mitten. It was shiny, silver, and lifeless again.

Kristy, pleased with this new toy, was in and out of the house in a flash. Jumping into the sleigh, she could feel her face light up like the moon above. Santa smiled and as he put the key away said, "My father was given that key by the elves one Christmas. The year before, he had a problem at a front door with his gigantic ring of master keys. He was fumbling with the key ring trying to find the right one for that type of lock. That was hard enough all by itself – the keys kept slipping, sliding, and dropping out of his clumsy, mittened hands. By this time, a doberman was bearing down on him from around the side of the house. The dog seemed mighty unhappy to see him. Dad found the right key but only by the seat of his pants, some of it still in the dog's mouth - thankfully now on the other side of the door."

Laughing, they were off again flying over towns, farms, and brightly lit cities, speeding away to deliver more holiday cheer to the sleeping children of the world. Kristy was filling up on the love that glowed so strongly this night. She could hardly sit still, like a helium balloon she strained at the end of her reins, lighter than air and anxious for the next stop.

Chapter 11

Nearing the Mediterranean and the equator it warmed considerably - gone now were the heavy parkas, the overgloves, and boots. Kristy felt freer as she flew. She could move her arms and legs with ease. She was dressed now in only slacks and a T-shirt, with light gloves and hooded jacket - at any rate, light by North Pole standards - and of course, all in red.

Flying lazily over another sea of clouds, the tail of an airplane, like the fin of a shark, cut a path in front of the reindeer. The reindeer spooked and took a sharp dive through the clouds. The sleigh and its passengers began to spin out of control. It dropped - tossing both passengers around like rag dolls in a clothes dryer. The reins tore from Kristy's hands.

With no one at the helm, the reindeer became confused and began to panic. At first, Kristy froze in shock as she sensed their fear. They needed her desperately. Kristy knew they soon would be hopelessly tangled. The only thing that would put an end to that would be a fatal crash into the ground.

Without a thought for her own safety, Kristy vaulted over the front of the sleigh to land on the back of Donder. She misjudged her jump and, landing off-center, began to slide off the left side of the reindeer. Grabbing at Donder's coat, Kristy gasped at the sight of a vast sea of sand spinning up to smash her. Donder used her antlers to push Kristy upright. Fighting the biting wind and the bucking and rocking animals, Kristy pulled herself to her feet on Donder's back then launched herself onto the back of Comet from which she hoped to reach the reins. She bit her lip as she landed with a jarring thump, but she ignored the pain and the taste of sweat and blood to stretch her arm out for the reins that were whipping in the wind. Willing her arm to stretch beyond its limit and unwilling to give up, Kristy wanted to cry with joy when she finally felt the reins slap into her hands. Pulling the reins tight calmed the team in an instant and soon she had them under control, but her corrections did not come soon enough. The rear of the blades struck the ground, hurling Santa into the bed of the sleigh and tangling the reindeer.

Santa fought off waves of pain as he rose from the back of the sleigh, where he had landed smack dab on top of the Santa Sack. The stabbing pains were again shooting down both legs. Still, he considered himself lucky to have landed safely and not been plunged to the ground.

Anxious about his daughter's safety he looked about for her and found her caressing and calming the reindeer.

He watched as, quick as lightning, she had untangled them from the tack and made sure that none of them were injured.

"Are you all right?"

"We're fine, Dad, just a few bumps and bruises." Turning to Comet she cooed, "Isn't that right, good buddy?"

How remarkably calm she is. When I first saw the look on her face when she lost the reins, I thought she would be frozen into immobility. I knew she needed me. I had to protect her. I was wrong. What a flight! What a save! Miraculous, marvelous, my daughter is a hero!

"That was terrific work, Kristy! I have never seen anything like it. I could not have done it better myself. You may just have saved Christmas for most of the world." That was what Santa wanted to say, what he should have said, but his dumb pride and stubbornness would not let him do it.

They flew in uncomfortable silence for a while as Kristy racked her brain for something, anything, to say to get them talking again. Finally, something occurred to her.

"Dad, I think I had another elf prank," Kristy said, "at the Karras place and worst of all - it maybe was caught on video."

"Is that why you came out of there fuming?" Santa answered. "You don't have to worry about any recording. The Santa Sack has elfin magic to disable any camera or video equipment unless you deactivate it."

"Anyway, little Leah Karras sent you a letter asking

for, and I quote: 'fishies in a bowl, and wood you pleas feed them four me so they do not go hugry. Lov Leah.'"

"I remember that one!"

"Well, I was expecting a fishbowl - you know about the size of a soccer ball!"

"A reasonable assumption."

"Anyway, as I neared the tree, the Santa Sack got heavier and heavier. I almost dropped it. When I opened the sack, lo and behold, there sat a rectangular tank. It was filled with water. It already had rocks in the bottom!"

Santa's laughter was beginning to shake the sleigh now.

"That's not all. It had three fish in it. When I put my hands on it to lift it out of the sack, a flash went off in my face!"

"Ho, ho, ho! That was the elfin magic, meant to hold the contents in during the trip." Most of his words were now coming out in gasps between chuckles.

Kristy frowned angrily at her father before she continued, "Anyway, I got it lifted and was trying to carry this slippery, cold tank over to the table nearest the tree. When I took a step to the right - the water began to slosh right. So, I took a small step to the left - the water sloshed left. I stopped to get the water settled and it sloshed into my face! Oh, that was awful – fish poop water, yuck! My arms were aching. I was scared I'd trip on the cords and hoses, or spill the tank and murder the fish. I didn't think I'd make those last slow steps, but I did! I made it to the table."

Santa just roared with laughter, "Those elves!"

Kristy thought about how she must have looked - red faced, sweaty, and wet. She felt better knowing it was not recorded.

"But, Dad, why would you ever want the cameras to record you?"

"Well, I sometimes deactivate it so that I can send a special video message to children who have been especially good that year."

The evening's warm glow returned to Kristy now that her father was speaking to her again.

Chapter 12

Somewhere over the ocean heading for South America, Santa said, "We are making great time. We must be about an hour, maybe two, ahead of schedule thanks to Chris's flight itinerary."

"Chris created it when he was bored in your geography class. He also invented the sleigh cup-holders and put in the heater as well."

Santa expressed his appreciation by bending over and warming his hands, "I really like this heater. I could have used it years ago. How did Christopher make this?"

"Dad," Kristy sighed, "Chris is the inventor not me. If you want the details, you ask him. I hate shop class. All I know is there's a hidden drawer under the glove compartment and three elvight."

Santa was wishing out loud when he asked, "Do you think Chris could invent one for the ground sleigh as well? I know at least two old elf drivers who would be mighty grateful if he could."

"You ask Chris to invent something for you and he'll be your friend for life," Kristy laughed.

The Christmas sleigh continued along its merry route over the Atlantic Ocean. Beneath them, a ruffled ribbon of moonlight lit a path across the water. Starlight was a mere vague shimmer on either side. The air was clear and crisp with a faint briny tinge.

Both the driver and the passenger were relaxed and comfortable. They were quiet for a moment as together they took in the billions of stars overhead.

"The stars look so different down here," sighed Kristy. The Milky Way shone so bright here with extra bursts of light and strange dark patches. It dazzled her.

"They are strange because the ones you know from home are upside down."

Kristy stood and bent over until she rested her head on the seat, "Wow, cool!"

"There are several star clusters down here you cannot see at home," Santa said. He pointed to one ahead of them, "That one is called 'Lupus, the Wolf.' I could never see it myself."

By squinting out of one eye, Kristy, wanting to believe, could just make out the shape of a wolf, but only with a lot of imagining.

"The easiest one to make out is the Southern Cross, so it is useful for finding out where we are down here.

"Kristine, put on your parka. It gets plenty cold in the Andes Mountains."

"That is North America up ahead," said Santa. The land they neared was haloed by lights that blocked out the stars just above.

"Wow," Kristy exclaimed, "look at all those lights! Does it ever get dark?"

"Not so much anymore," Santa said, "most of the people there never properly see the beauty of the heavens. They're in the dark about the dark."

The tone of his voice made Kristy sad. She could not imagine a world that never saw the stars.

"You could say," Kristy recited,

> "City night, city bright
> "No star I see tonight,
> "I wish to know, I wish I might,
> "See what a starry sky is like."

The ho, ho, hos rolled out of Santa as he laughed.

Kristy and Santa began their flight over the mass of lights. Waves of frothy surf broke against the massed bulk of thousands of dark, solid shapes that lined the shore. The lights from millions of windows gave form to the building blocks, while strings of streetlights outlined courses that Kristy itched to race along. She did not even have to look at her father to know that using those lighted streets as a racetrack would not be allowed. Kristy reined in her excitement.

They visited home after home up the Florida peninsula, then headed west to begin their zigzag journey across the United States. From California, they flew across the Pacific Ocean to Hawaii. Back again, they flew to California, then across the country to the Atlantic seaboard. Stopping at every house, shack, or apartment where some child was expecting a visit from Santa.

They crossed Virginia and were busy changing from light jackets to winter. They were far enough north of the equator now that the air at their elevation was more than just a little nippy. While struggling to get their arms into their sleeves, Santa and Kristy lost track of their location.

A United States Air Force tech watching her screen sat up straight - instantly alert. In the time it takes for just one heartbeat, she grabbed the phone, "I have a small, fast-moving, unidentified flying object entering restricted air space over D.C."

"What?" a voice screamed in her ear. She hung up the phone when it went dead and continued to stare in alarm at the unauthorized blinking dot. Overhead she heard the orders to scramble.

Back in the night sky, Kristy and Santa were about to land on the next house on their list. Out of nowhere, two Air Force fighter jets roared into position, soaring by one on either side of the sleigh. Santa jumped and Kristy nearly wet her pants.

Santa yelled over the jet engine noise, "That darn coat made me forget – there's a No-Fly Zone over Washington!"

"A what? What will we do now, Dad?"

"We do our job."

He pointed to the mansion below them. The jets were

making their second pass when Santa and Kristy waved a cheerful good-bye to the pilots. Shock was written on the part of the pilots' faces visible around their masks.

Kristy pushed the sleigh into a nosedive leaving the two jets in mid-air alone. The jets circled off to make another pass of the sleigh. Santa grabbed tight to his seat. Kristy was a ball of energy. She threw herself into overdrive and passed her excitement onto the reindeer with three quick clicks of her tongue. Now, Kristy did what she had been dreaming of since she first spotted the miles of glowing racetracks called roads beneath her. She blasted around the Capital dome, throwing Santa almost out of the sleigh. She was a flying Indy driver now! They soared down the Mall with snow kicking up a smoke screen behind them. Kristy turned three tight spirals around the Washington Monument then landed the sleigh as quietly as a snowflake on the roof of 1600 Pennsylvania Avenue. With a greenish tinge to his face, Santa hoisted himself up from the floor of the sleigh and dropped back into the seat.

"I wish now I had eaten fewer cookies."

The pilots pulled their jets up to circle overhead. Frank watched mesmerized as below them the tiny sleigh that had out-flown them settled down with its red-clothed driver and eight tiny reindeer.

A voice came over his headset, "It just dropped off the radar screen. Did you see what it was?"

Frank, thinking of his kids back home, snuggled in

their warm beds, replied to the voice on the headset, "I didn't see anything, did you Bart?"

"Not a thing."

A rough voice barked in his headset, "What do you mean? It was right between the two of you. You had to see something."

Frank gave Bart a thumbs-up and flew off back to base.

Santa caught his breath as he and Kristy looked out from a rooftop bristling with chimneys, antennae, and surveillance equipment, "Sorry, I forgot to tell you we have to fly low around the D.C. area, *under* the radar."

Kristy stood up in the sleigh and watched the jets disappear into the night sky. She was shaking with anger but also excitement and was trying to control her temper, "Reindeer poop! Thanks for that little bit of info, Dad."

"Language, Kristine!"

Uniformed men bristling with weapons suddenly surrounded them. The man with the most ribbons stepped up to the sleigh, "You're early, Santa."

Chapter 13

Except for the short spell of bad weather they had over Kansas, the rest of the trip had gone well. The night was mostly clear at their flight level and the moon and stars shone and twinkled above. Flying over the occasional cottony sea of white clouds was almost like being home at the North Pole. They sipped hot cocoa, sang Christmas carols, and told each other their adventures. Kristy was thrilled to tell her father about her visit to each house. Santa listened, smiled, and nodded his head. He drew on stories from decades of deliveries. As Kristy listened, she began to see through her father's eyes. She puffed up with pride. Her family, her dad, did all this.

Kristy entered another quiet home brightly lit with all the colors and feelings of Christmas. She put five presents under the Christmas tree then moved across the floor to the stockings hanging by the stairs. She filled all six of the socks with little presents and candy canes. She looked back at the beautifully wrapped presents under the tree, then back to the stockings.

Kristy poked her hand into the Santa Sack feeling all

around. Quick as a rabbit she was off to the sleigh where her father was checking the harness on the reindeer.

In a panicked voice, Kristy shouted, "Dad, I'm missing a present."

Santa looked puzzled as he peered into the velvet bag. "What do you mean?"

"Six children live at this house, Dad. I put only five presents under their tree. I need six and the gifts for this house are used up. Rebecca still needs a present!"

"We had all the Gift Magic when we left the North Pole. One must have fallen out somewhere, possibly over the desert when we were nearly wiped out by that airplane."

"But, Dad, that's on the other side of the world and anyway, how can we bring back lost magic?"

"Not possible."

"We can't just go to the store and get a new one, all the stores are closed. We don't have time to go back home and get a new gift," Kristy's voice rose even higher, "What are we going to do?"

Santa sat back in his seat, "First, we don't panic. Second, we use our brains."

Remembering some instructions Chris had given her earlier, Kristy said, "This is an emergency, isn't it?"

"Well, if this isn't an emergency, I don't know what is."

Kristy pointed to the first aid kit at Santa's feet.

"It's bigger than usual," Santa said.

"Open it and hand me the e-phone."

"The what?"

"It looks like a normal cell phone. Chris calls it the 'e-phone.' It's a two-way phone to the North Pole. He said to use it only in case of emergency."

Santa looked stunned but he handed her the e-phone. Then he carefully pulled out grandpa's antique globe.

He inspected it closely, "Something has been done to this also! Christopher has tinkered with the globe I used for decades to guide my sleigh. What is this wire for?" he asked, fingering a cord running to the elvight heater. "And what is this blinking, blue light?"

"That's Chris's G.P.S. He can track us with that. He knows exactly where we are at all times."

Kristy was alarmed as her father's face turned a furious, fiery red. He grabbed the phone.

Back in Santa's office at the North Pole, Chris sat in his father's big, soft chair wrapped in a warm, woolen blanket. The glowing elvight fire in a potbellied stove kept the room toasty warm. A mug of cocoa sat steaming on the desk near his laptop. From here, he followed the progress of the sleigh as it traveled over the face of the earth. Lately, his attention had wandered and now he was deep in thought on how he could hook up cameras to the sleigh and view Santa's progress back at home. He jumped when the e-phone rang.

"Hello, Chris here. Is there some sort of a problem, Kristy?"

"I don't know what you were thinking Christopher," Santa's hard voice said, "but we will have a long talk when I get back home."

"But, Dad," Chris argued, "I had to send Kristy in my

place. We here all know you have the right Santa sitting beside you. You see, I'm afraid of heights. That's why I can't..."

"Get over it," Santa said. He was shouting now, "You are going to be Santa, not Kristine, and as for your flying skills young man. You have a whole year to work on them."

"Here," Santa said, "You talk to him."

Kristy came on the line.

Chris rubbed tears from his eyes as he listened to Kristy's problem with the missing present. Chris told her to stay on their current course and he would get back to them after he met with Mom and Essen.

After hanging up, Chris grabbed a microphone. His voice rang out from speakers all over the compound, "Attention, attention, we have an emergency. Will Emma Claus and Essen please come to Santa's office at once?"

He repeated his message then put the mic down. Ten minutes later found the three of them grouped around Santa's desk throwing ideas back and forth. Their first idea was to send a lone reindeer with the gift, but the reindeer would need a driver. Chris really wished he were not afraid of heights. They thought of Mrs. Claus, but she was too big.

Essen's idea was to tie two reindeer to Mrs. Claus's feet. Emma glared at Essen and said, "When pigs fly, I'll try that nutty plan. How about you, will you try it?"

"Elves make toys and elves tend reindeer," Essen answered rather tightly, "but elves do not fly."

Then the gears began to turn in Chris's brain, "That's it – a toy!"

Running through the door, he yelled back over his shoulder, "Meet me in the electronic toy shop."

Chris flew through the house to his bedroom and grinned up at one special toy hanging from the ceiling. It was his black, four-foot remote controlled jet airplane – the pride and joy of his toy making skills. He carefully unhooked it and raced out to the shop.

At the shop, Chris told everyone his plan. Emma flew back to Santa's office to give the details to Kristy and Santa.

"Emma?" Santa asked.

"Hello, Kris, I don't have much time to talk, they need my help. Chris has a plan. He and the elves are in the shop working on it. First, you and Kristy need to change your route. Chris wants you to take a 500-mile northeast circle back to St. Louis."

She told him of Chris's toy jet plan, "I've got to go. We'll call you back soon."

Emma gave him no chance to ask questions. She hung up.

Emma rose and went over to the filing cabinet. She rifled through the file of all the children's wish lists. One drawer contained the lists mailed to Santa, one held a folder of those e-mailed to Santa, and one drawer was full of folders collected at the stores by Santa's helpers. She located the list that Rebecca had forwarded through Santa Ed, who had been helping the Clauses for years in St. Louis. Emma grabbed the list and tore off to the shop with it.

Chris and several shop elves bent over a table like surgeons performing a delicate operation on the toy plane laying open before them. They had already removed any extra parts not needed for this flight. The jet needed to be light to have room for Rebecca's toy.

Emma ran in with two wrapped gifts clutched in her arms, "I checked her list for the smallest items she asked for. I grabbed this movie and one mystic eight ball. I hope one of them fits in your plane."

"Thanks for your help, Mom. We had better send the movie. There's enough room and it weighs less."

She smiled at him then frowned at the jet, "How will you get this contraption all the way to St. Louis without running out of fuel?"

"Or running into something?" Essen asked.

"I don't have time for questions now. I'll tell you later."

Chris finished stowing the present in the plane. Essen, with Sam's help, took the plane outside for takeoff. Chris and his mother raced to Santa's office.

He explained to her as he sat behind the desk, "I put a global tracking device into the jet and I've been borrowing space on certain satellites all night."

Emma gasped, "Good glory, is that legal?"

She let out a long sigh, "Okay, Christopher, do what you must."

"I will fly and track the plane by watching that dot on my laptop," he pointed to the screen with a map of North America. A blue dot further north sat at the North Pole.

"First, we'll fly south along the 90th longitude over

Hudson's Bay. That way we avoid a lot of major cities."

He saw his mother's eyes grow large, "Don't worry. I'll fly below the full-sized jets and high enough to avoid tall buildings, trees, and power lines."

Concentrating now, Chris said quietly, "That just leaves small, private planes and drones. There shouldn't be many of them, it being Christmas Eve and all."

Emma pulled a chair up beside Chris and watched as the tiny blue dot began to move slowly down the screen. A red dot inched its way toward the curved line that marked longitude 90 degrees. She pointed to the screen.

"You are going to fly the jet, which is the blue dot, until it meets up with Kristy and Papa, the red dot."

"You got it, Mom. We're going to turn you into a computer geek yet."

His mother pulled a face, "Good glory, heaven help us!"

"For power, I used a mixture of jet fuel and elfin magic dust that I have been experimenting with. I never had time to work out how many miles per gallon I'll get, but..." and here Chris crossed his fingers behind his back.

Under his breath he muttered, "It could be very close."

Emma slouched in her chair, "I hoped it would be easier than this."

On his laptop, Chris pulled up a weather map to help him fly the jet. A team of very excited elves had worked rapidly to get Christopher's jet off the ground and headed south. All through Canada, it flew without a problem, just a little snow here and there. Just north of Thunder Bay the jet hit a patch of bad weather.

Chris knew the jet, hammered by blowing snow, was being tossed around in the wild wind. Flying around the storm would not work - it was too big. Time flew also. He had to make up his mind now!

He did not realize he was speaking out loud when he said, "To climb higher over the storm means burning up more fuel and leaving the jet short of its target. I can stay at this elevation and head straight through the storm. Will the toy hold together? If the jet falls apart over this isolated area, Santa and Kristy will have to fly miles out of their way to locate the presents in a land of towering pine trees and deep snow."

Poor little Rebecca sleeping in her bed, dreaming of presents on Christmas morning, then finding nothing. I cannot have that.

He knew what he had to do and punched the keys of his computer. He sent the plane up over the cold, winter clouds heading for its target - a small sleigh pulled by eight flying reindeer and in it, a not-quite jolly man with his unhappy daughter.

Kristy popped out of a chimney and gave her father a worried look.

"Dad, this is almost the last town before we get back on schedule and we have only a couple dozen homes left."

Santa slid over to make room for her beside him, "I have heard nothing from them since you left, I'm..." Just then, the e-phone lit up. Both passengers jumped for it. Santa got there first.

"Yo, ho, ho, ho," Santa answered, then he seemed to remember their troubles and frowned at the phone, "it's been a long time between calls."

Kristy grabbed the phone, "What took you so long?"

Chris said, "I'll tell you what later, but right now I need you two to head north by northwest as fast as you can and stay close to the ground."

Kristy took off and flew as instructed. She kept the phone close.

"My jet is running out of fuel," Chris explained. Kristy heard the concern in his voice. She knew how much that jet plane meant to him. How much it would hurt him to lose it.

Santa cut into her thoughts by yelling into the phone, "How are we going to find that tiny jet in all these clouds?"

"I attached a flare to the plane and wired it into the battery just in case. It's not a very big one. Can't let it set the jet on fire. We need to get the jet and sleigh as close together as possible. When your dot on my computer meets the jet's dot heading south, I will hit the F1 key and ignite the flare."

As Kristy filled her father in, things got a little worse - it began to snow heavily. Santa and Kristy were beginning to lose hope. Suddenly out of the corner of her eye, Kristy saw a flash of blue light off to her left. She turned the sleigh so hard it almost knocked Santa over the side. Kristy watched closely as Chris's jet began to spiral down toward the open waters of the Mississippi River.

The reindeer pulled with all their might and Kristy flew like the ace pilot she always knew she could be. Dipping sharply down, she moved the sleigh beneath the falling jet and matched its angling descent. The runners had just skimmed the surface of the river when the toy jet crashed onto the Santa Sack in the rear of the sleigh.

Santa sighed with relief and relaxed back into the seat as Kristy, driven by guilt at losing the present in the first place, raced like the driven snow toward St. Louis. She was determined to get back to Rebecca's before the children woke up to discover anything missing.

Chapter 14

After a quick and successful stop at Rebecca's, a few dozen more cookies and gallons of milk, Kristy headed the sleigh to the last village of the night. As they circled one rooftop, Kristy noticed there was smoke rising from the chimney. She looked with some concern at her father who scowled back.

"Well, get on with it," he said and roughly pushed her in the direction of the chimney.

"But, Dad, it's still lit."

Santa squinted at the chimney a moment then nodded, "It sure is." Then he removed his glove and rummaged in his parka pocket.

"Most people remember that I'm coming and put the fire out so it's good and cold when I get here. Ah, here it is."

Santa withdrew a leather bag closed with a rawhide string. Pulling the bag open, he reached in and drew out something small and black. He motioned for Kristy to open her hand. Onto her mitten, he dropped a tiny object for her to take. When she raised it up to her nose, she saw a small, round pill the size and shape of an aspirin but entirely black and with an unpleasant, burnt-toast odor.

"Fireplug," Santa said, and he grandly brushed his hands together as if to indicate that that was that, that it was simple, and that was all there was to it. "Throw it down the chimney and then wait five seconds before you jump down."

Kristy closed her hand tightly around the Fireplug and crunched across the snow to the chimney. She turned her face away from the rising smoke. She stood back far enough to reach her hand over the chimney while keeping the smoke out of her eyes. When she judged her hand to be in the proper position, she turned it over and shook it to send the pill down into the dark.

One thousand one, one thousand two, one thousand three, one thousand four, one thousand five, Kristy counted to herself. She faced the chimney and lo and behold – no smoke. The air was no longer warm, and it smelled clean. Kristy grinned happily at her father before she took a deep breath and dropped down the chimney.

Sitting alone in the sleigh Santa looked at his father's magical location device.

So, this tracked us all night long. He ran his hand over the eight-inch globe. It amazed him--how the elves could have made it. The globe hovered beneath the hand of a golden arm, bent at the elbow, and attached by the shoulder to the sleigh. One finger of the stationary hand pointed to their position on the rotating globe.

Christopher would call it inexact and unscientific.

Santa sighed. He slid the top half of the globe into the bottom to reveal an elegantly crafted compass. On a snowy or cloudy night, it was the only way to know where Polaris and north was. It always pointed the way home.

Of course, Christopher already has it in mind to replace it with something much more modern. That boy has no respect for tradition.

The globe always reminded Santa of his father. He recalled the many times his father left on Christmas Eve leaving him behind and how he had longed to join Santa on his yearly mission.

That is just what Kristy said earlier, he remembered.

He closed the globe and poured some more cocoa into his mug. As he wrapped his cold fingers around the cup, the steam rose to warm his chilled face.

Looking down into the swirling milk recalled many a night delivering presents in weather just as turbulent. The reindeer pawing at the snow on the roof drew his attention away from his thoughts. Kristy had become so efficient, so reliable, that for the first time tonight he had the leisure to enjoy the panoramic snow-filled Christmas scene before him. Holiday lights twinkled softly through the falling snow while smoke from the chimneys rose to soften the glow of the streetlights below. It sank in for Santa just how much he was going to miss these special moments and how lucky he was to have a job that brought him so much love and joy. He thought with a bittersweet feeling that all his ancestors must have felt this exact same way on their last night. A couple of tears slipped onto Santa's cheeks and froze.

Santa's memories were interrupted by voices wafting

up the chimney. Not one voice - not just Kristy's voice - but several voices! He eased himself out of the sleigh and carefully quietly approached the chimney.

After leaving the fireplace, Kristy found a nativity set holding pride of place under the Christmas tree. She couldn't take the time to study it, however, because she knew her time was short. She lay the presents under the tree softly. She did not want to disturb the porcelain figures around the crèche. She turned to look for the cookies. Kristy nearly jumped out of her boots. Two children, Jacob and Kylie, were standing at the bottom of a flight of stairs.

With excitement Jacob squeaked, "I toll you I hewed Santa Claus. I toll you. I toll you."

Kylie wiped the sleep from her eyes with the hand of her teddy bear, "That's not Santa Claus. It's a girl."

The boy peered more closely at Kristy, "When you doing in our house? Awe you stealing ouw pwesents?"

"He means *what* are you doing in our house?" Kylie interpreted.

Kristy forced a grin onto her face, hoping to avoid a loud argument that could involve parents, "I am Santa, at least for tonight."

"Prove it!" Kylie demanded.

"Santa, my dad, is up on the roof in the sleigh. I'm learning on the job." Kristy held up the Santa Sack as evidence.

"If you're Santa's daughter," the girl questioned, "then

tell me how you got in here."

"I can't," Kristy replied, "that's a Santa Secret."

"Can weindeew weally fly?" Jacob asked.

"Ours do."

With barely a pause for the answer, the boy continued, "Do you live at the Nowf Pole?"

"Of course, we do."

"Then how come nobody ever found your house?" Kylie grilled Kristy.

Kristy thought hard for an answer that would satisfy this critical child. "It's hidden – from above and all around. Santa's home and workshops blend in with the snow and ice. And a little elf magic doesn't hurt."

"Elves," the boy sighed, "did they make my pwesent? When is my pwesent?'

"I can't tell you. It's a surprise. You must wait until you wake up in the morning and open it."

Kylie, still looking doubtful, slyly asked, "If you can't tell me what my present is this year, tell me: what did I get last year?"

That put Kristy into a panic. How could she remember what one little girl got last year?

A deep, male voice rang out of the fireplace, "You received a pink, hooded sweater and a porcelain doll in a purple, lacy dress with a big straw hat and a parasol."

Jacob gasped and his sister was shocked into silence. The boy ran to the fireplace and shouted up the chimney, "Tanks for the pwesent, Santa," and he ran up the stairs toward bed.

Kylie running after him, paused on the landing, turned to Kristy, and said, "Do you think that someday I could be Santa Claus too?"

What could Kristy say to that? On the one hand, the girl seemed so hopeful. On the other, it did look like even a daughter of Santa Claus could never become Santa. Kristy hid a bitter smile behind her mitten as she answered, "You never know. Anything is possible."

"Wow, thanks," said the child and she bounded up the stairs after her brother.

Kristy popped out of the chimney, walked around the reindeer, caressing and hugging each of them. She knew that her time was ending. Kristy climbed back into the sleigh. Her father turned to her with a peaceful but sad expression and said, "There is only one house left. Do you mind if I handle things just one last time?"

"Oh, Dad, I don't mind."

Kristy now knew what her father was feeling. She was feeling a heavy sense of loss herself at never experiencing the Christmas magic again. If her loss was so painful after just one night, what must his be like after a lifetime?

Chapter 15

T he snow was about a foot deep and covered with a thin coating of ice on the roof of the last house of the night. The reindeer hooves and the runners of the sleigh landed gingerly this last time. The snow made a loud, cracking noise underneath.

Santa let out a rough moan as he turned to get out. He gripped the dashboard of the sleigh tightly with his mittens. Kristy, seeing her father in pain, carefully jumped out and slid around the sleigh to help him.

With a grimace on his face, he asked Kristy, "I don't suppose Chris has a walker built into the sleigh?"

Santa leaned on Kristy as his boots crunched through the snow with every step he took. As soon as he seemed to be going along well, Kristy let go, and instantly her father was off. She watched helplessly as he slid down the roof arms flailing around. He slid only about four feet, but he came to a hard and abrupt stop. With his legs up in the air resting on the side of the chimney and his back flat on the roof, he yelled up to Kristy, "Luckily I hit the chimney, or I might have really hurt myself."

He laughed aloud then groaned in pain. Kristy grabbed the Santa Sack and skated carefully down to help her father right himself. Santa took the bag and accepted Kristy's help to climb onto the chimney. By leaning on his daughter and with a bit of grunting, he was able to hoist his legs over the side. Then he rested a moment, taking slow careful breaths. Santa took his final 'descend' breath and slipped over the edge.

The moment Santa landed in the fireplace he was stuck.

I cannot squat. I cannot bend. I cannot get out of this fireplace.

He tilted his head up to see his daughter looking down at him.

"I could really use your help. I am stuck down here."

Kristy thought for a few seconds, climbed back up to the sleigh, jumped in, and swooped it off the roof to land near the back door. She grabbed the Skeleton Key before scrunching her way through the snow to the door. Letting herself into the house, she passed through the kitchen, searching for the living room. She located it at the end of a short hallway. The fireplace was in the wall to her left.

Kristy nearly gagged on the laughter she had to hold back at the sight of her father's bottom half in the fireplace with a cat licking his boots. Racing over to the fireplace, she shooed the cat off. It hissed and swatted at her before it ran out of the room.

Kristy kneeled and looked up at her father in the fireplace. She was puzzled for a moment - he had plenty of room.

"Kristy, are you going to help me or are you just going to sit there?"

"Dad, just bend your knees."

"Don't you think I've tried that?"

Kristy chuckled to herself then an idea hit her. She stood up, grabbed hold of the back of her father's boots and backed up pulling them out towards the living room. She winced when she heard his head hit the back of the chimney and bounce off a brick as he slid down the back wall of the fireplace.

Now his back was flat on the floor, his boots in the living room, and just his head remained in the fireplace. Kristy watched her father anxiously as he opened his eyes and slowly, gingerly shook his head. She was feeling more than a little guilty for not having warned him before she pulled the legs out from under him. She hoped he was not badly hurt.

Straightening his cap as Kristy helped him up once again, his face twitched with a weak attempt at a smile. He mumbled a thank you, patted his ample stomach and rounded butt, and said, "Luckily Mama keeps me well padded."

Laughing but trying desperately to remain quiet, they leaned against each other until they regained control.

Back in command of himself, Santa moved stiffly while he filled the stockings. Kristy surveyed the room. She could tell that a decorator lived in this house. The stockings were blue velveteen with white, felt snowflake appliqués. They matched the fragile Christmas tree decorated in shades of blue with white accents.

Kristy stood back and lent a hand only when asked. She watched her father remove six presents wrapped in blue and white paper with white or blue bows from the

Santa Sack, and slowly, carefully place them under the matching Christmas tree. Figuring it was his last delivery and that he probably wanted to stretch it out as long as possible, Kristy waited patiently for him to finish.

Near the tree sat a small, round table, covered by a blue and white quilted tablecloth. On the table precisely arranged were a glass of milk, a plate of cookies, and a note. Santa read the note as he ate the cookies and drank the milk. Kristy watched in some surprise as her father began to blink back tears. Without a word, he handed her the note. In big, sloppy letters, a child had written:

Dear Santa: If you have any presents for us, please take them to Oscar Renquist. He had a fire at his house yesterday. He needs them more than we do and he was better than us anyway. We know you can do this even though we did not tell you sooner, because it's Christmas and you are Santa Claus.

Love, Josh and Billy

Kristy glanced at the Christmas tree and was not very surprised to see that there were now only two Santa presents under the tree – not 'none', like Josh and Billy had asked, but two. Santa beamed at her as he held out the Santa Sack tugged three times on the cord and turned to face a camera sitting on the mantle. A red light began to blink.

"Ho, ho, ho," said Santa as Kristy watched over his shoulder, "Josh and Billy, you have been especially good for thinking of Oscar. "

The Santa Sack was bumpy again. With Josh and Billy's presents going to Oscar. Santa pulled the cord three times, and the camera grew dark.

"One more stop?" she asked.

Her father just nodded and said, "Oscar was not a believer, but he is now on the itinerary, thanks to Josh and Billy. It will be our last stop."

"He will be a believer in the morning."

Santa glanced over at the fireplace, straightened his suit and then his shoulders. He had already taken a deep breath before Kristy realized he was getting ready for a painful rise back up the chimney.

Kristy whispered to her father, "Dad, I have the sleigh out back."

Her father smiled at her, and Kristy thought she saw tears of thanks in his eyes before he turned and strolled towards the door while rubbing the back of his head.

Chapter 16

Santa took the reins after the Renquist house. He uttered not a word on their flight back to the North Pole. Kristy stole glances at her father, but she never caught him looking at her. He stared straight ahead and chewed on his mustache. She closed her mouth and kept silent.

I'm not surprised he's mad. We sure put him through a lot tonight. We upset all his plans.

The snow and ice below continued with only minor variations in height and texture and color for many miles. It was hard to tell where they were, but a dry, heavy lump in Kristy's stomach told her they were nearly home. She glanced quickly at the globe. The blue light had disappeared under the bronze cap that connected the arm to the globe. Next to her, Santa whistled two short notes to the reindeer and they began their last descent for the night.

From above, she could see there was no way to tell where the real North Pole lay. The drifts of snow covered their home in white blankets.

We are nearly home, and this is the end of my dream. I

will always be proud of the job I did. I made a great Santa.

The grey-white ground was rapidly rising to meet them. The reindeer leveled off. Then the light in the barn became visible to the right and the lights of home on the left. She remembered last year watching Santa land, so she knew the reindeer would glide toward the right - to the barn for food and much needed rest. They landed gently on the packed snow as the barn doors were opened by two field elves.

Once inside, Santa threw the reins to her and barked, "Finish up in here." Then he limped off in the direction of the house and the annual welcome home and Christmas party.

For a couple of minutes Kristy just sat in the sleigh with the reins lying limp in her hands. The elves said not a word as they freed the reindeer from the traces and led them away. Her mind replayed the night: the silent flight in the sleigh. She saw carpets of billowy, white clouds below and the sharp, bright stars above so close she wanted to reach out and pluck one from the sky. Images of wrapped and decorated presents left for sleeping, peaceful children to squeal over in the morning made her hands feel empty. She had been part of something wonderful.

That's why Dad is so upset. He will miss it all too.

A long, wavering sigh forced its way from Kristy's throat. She refused to give in to tears. She was going to finish her job so well that her father would never be able to shame her with it. She threw back her shoulders, lifted her chin and jumped out of the sleigh. Kristy walked with head held high to the center of the barn. She caught a pitchfork flung to her by a grinning field elf and spread the feed for the circling reindeer.

As they worked, Kristy could tell by the elves' various expressions that something unusual was going on somewhere at the North Pole. Once or twice, the elves paused as if straining to hear something. When one caught her looking in his direction, he grinned and gave her a thumbs-up. Donnau, a quiet elf who had said no more than two words to Kristy before, broke into a speech.

"We all know how strong and brave you are. You are a genius with reindeer – better even than your mother is. Oh, and the way you can fly!"

At one point all the elves paused, eyebrows raised. They stared at each other open-mouthed. Dropping their heads, as if embarrassed, they went quickly back to work.

The reindeer acted skittish, as if they sensed danger. They circled Kristy as if she was one of their fawns, needing protection. She held out her hands and brushed their backs as they passed. Kristy felt they were trying to say they loved her. It comforted her.

"We'll get you all fed and settled," she murmured as she rubbed her cheek along Dancer's neck. Kristy's smile was thin, but not forced. She brushed tears from her face and then from Dancer's coat. Kristy knew Dancer hated to have boogers in her coat.

"I'm going to the party now and pretend it is being given for me. For me - the best Santa there ever was."

Chapter 17

Chris surveyed the eerily quiet workroom. The large room, cleared for the annual party, seemed flat. Red and green bunting hung in twisted rows from wall to wall. Above that the elvight flowed in a Northern Lights show of their own. Holly, ivy, and plenty of evergreen boughs decorated the doors and the platform serving as a stage. Tables groaned under the weight of food - meat (including three types of sausage with sauerkraut), sixteen potato dishes, half a dozen goulashes, dozens of salads, and sweets from all over the world. Only the noise was missing. No glasses clinked. No laughter tickled the ear. No music played to prove that a party was about to begin.

He smiled at two young elves, Hortense and Kibble, who stood either side of the main doors. Chosen for the honor of ushering Santa into the room, they wore their finest clothes. Sam and Essen were giving them last-minute instructions on the ceremony. Sam's loud and forceful directions caused the field elf, Kibble, to shake in his pointed shoes. Hortense, who worked for Essen, casually checked the state of her teeth and the wave of her hair in the reflection on the shiny, brass doorknob.

Chris turned his cup of punch round and round in his hands. Beside him, his mother silently sipped at her eggnog. Normally relief that another year of planning and toil were over made her lips move as fast as humming-bird wings - but not tonight. They exchanged worried and unhappy looks.

The elf band struck a chord and swung into "Santa Claus Is Coming to Town". That was the signal. Santa was on his way from the barn.

"Good glory, but he's early," Emma said and there was a shake in her voice.

Hortense and Kibble straightened their tunics and swallowed hard. They pressed their pointy ears to the door as instructed but that was a mistake. They had no time to leap out of the way before Santa burst through the doors. The doors swung shut in Santa's wake leaving Hortense and Kibble each stuck by an ear, like a suction cup on glass, to the wooden doors.

Chris knew they were in for it now. His father, nev-er one to ignore tradition, had just tossed two hundred years of it out the window when he entered without the honored elves' introduction.

Santa glowered at his wife then pointed to the carved oaken door to his office. She swallowed and cleared her throat before handing Chris her cup and following in Santa's wake. When Chris moved to join them, Santa's hard look shouted,

"No."

The door had barely slammed shut behind them when the eruption began. Santa stopped before his desk and spun to face her.

"How could you?" he fumed, and the volume of his voice cranked up a notch. "How could you do this to me? I always thought that you would be on my side!"

"I am on your side," Emma said. She spoke as softly as she could in an effort to calm him. She could only reason with a calm Santa.

"Then why did you go behind my back and join up with the children against me?" Now Santa was shouting.

Emma tried a gentler tone, but she had to raise her voice to break through to her husband, "I am not *against* you."

"No. What would you call it then?"

"Opening your eyes," Emma said quietly, "sometimes you are just blind to anything that does not fall into your traditions."

"Tradition has served this family well for many a generation."

"So have family loyalty, love and respect."

Santa sputtered for a moment. His face turned red as he replied, "But not toward me?"

"Kris, we all love and respect you and we tried to talk to you, but you just would not listen. We just wanted you to see what the children are capable of."

"*That* you accomplished, and you nearly ruined Christmas!"

"Ruined!" Now Emma began shouting too, "Christmas was never in any danger from us. Chris is fully able to run the toy shops and I am perfectly capable of overseeing the tasks I set for him. Kristy is already in the top five of the best pilots this family has ever produced – *and she was with you!*"

Emma calmed herself with a slow, deep breath and continued more quietly, "Our only way to reach you was to show you."

Emma folded her husband into her arms and held him quietly for a moment before she spoke, "Oh, Kris, I know how much this job has meant to you. I am not blind. I have seen the look on your face each Christmas Eve when you take off and especially the brilliant one you wear when you return. No matter how trying the journey, no matter how tired and worn, you were always glowing with joy and pride. Your bliss was evident. I do understand your anger and bitterness."

Santa searched for something in her eyes and seeming to find it said, "Yes, I guess you do. But I do not think you understand about the legacy."

"You still have a legacy," Emma whispered, "a double legacy. Chris will gladly assume your role as toymaker and Kristy...."

"Kristy!" Santa shouted.

Chapter 18

Chris froze in his slippers as he stared at the door his mother and father had just slammed shut. He would have remained his mother's stiff cup-holder, if a helpful shop elf had not come to relieve him of his burden.

From behind closed doors, the voices of Santa and Mom were raised in angry dispute. Chris chewed his nails, at words like deceit, respect, and tradition. When the noise became murmurs, Chris noticed he was not his parents' only audience. All the elves in the room stood still. Considering the unique design of their ears, they had probably heard more than he had.

Chris knew where to go for the most reliable news. He wove his way through tables, chairs, and wide-eyed elves to Sam and Essen, busy peeling Hortense and Kibble off the doors.

"Sam," Chris said with as much command as his twelve-year-old voice could manage. Essen excused himself and ran off. Hortense and Kibble backed as far away as they could without leaving their posts and turned their ears in another direction.

"Son," Sam answered in a firm tone that clearly indicated he was not to be intimidated.

Chris tried anyway.

"Tell me what they are saying behind that door," he demanded.

Sam crossed his arms and looked up at Chris with a stern frown. His lips were zipped tight.

"Well, can you at least tell me how bad it is?" He whined.

Sam listened intently while he cracked the knuckles of each hand. Finally, he looked at Chris with a face slightly less stern. Chris thought it could be a smile.

"Your father is letting off steam."

Glancing fearfully at the door, Chris said "Steam! Sounds like a volcano."

He was not sure if Sam was agreeing when he nodded very slowly. Sam squinted back at Santa's office door, listening closely. Knowing from hard experience that Sam was not an elf to be rushed, Chris waited, chewing his nail.

"Your father feels that his useful life is over. He is fighting to hold on by insisting that events proceed in the 'proper' order."

"What do you mean his useful life is over? He has lots to do," Chris objected. "He has to continue to train the next Santa. He's still needed.

"I'm good with toys, but I've never been in charge. I'm not ready to run the whole show. If by some miracle he chooses Kristy, heck, she's not ready. It's only been one night! He can't possibly have taught her everything he knows tonight."

Pointy elf ears suddenly perked up and their heads turned in unison toward the grand double doors where Hortense and Kibble stood. The band struck up the first three notes of "Santa Claus is Coming to Town" but whistled and twanged to a halt as they stared at each other in confusion.

Santa burst from his office and shouted, "Bar the door!"

Hortense and Kibble nearly tripped over themselves as they rushed to obey. The bar dropped in place just as something soft but solid crashed into it.

"Hey," Kristy shouted from the other side of the door, "What's the big idea? Chris, let me in or I'll dye your underpants pink."

The elves looked to Santa for an answer. Chris looked to his mother. Emma, paler than ever Chris had seen her, gestured with a finger over her lips for him to keep silent. His throat tightened and a terrible dread filled his heart as his sister began to pound on the door and call for help.

Santa spoke quietly to the band then went to the door for a discussion with Sam, Essen, Hortense, and Kibble. He went up to the stage and waved for Chris to join him.

"This is not funny, Dad, you ate all the cookies remember. I'm still hungry," yelled Kristy from the hallway.

Chris could hear tears in her voice. He could barely hold in a fit of rage he was certain would blow the roof off, when his mother squeezed his hand. She smiled a tight, tiny smile at him and nodded toward his father.

From behind the door a voice whined, "Mom."

Chris didn't know how it could be possible, but his father was enjoying this. Santa grinned from ear to ear as he nodded at the band.

Finally, and loudly, the band broke into "*S*anta Claus is Coming to Town" - this time without stop. From their places by the door, Hortense and Kibble bowed, drew the bolt on the doors, swung them open and shouted over the music, "Another successful Christmas Eve flight. Let the party begin."

"Hip, hip, hoorah!" Sam began and all the elves, Santa, Emma, and Chris joined in, "hip, hip, hoorah!"

On the third round, Kristy smiled and joined in too. Santa and Mom laughed at that. Chris looked confused.

Santa waved for her to join the family on the stage.

Arriving next to Chris, she asked him, "What in reindeer poop is going on?"

"Dad returned in a rage. Mom and Dad had it out in the office. That's all I know. Hush!"

"I know you are all expecting a fine speech about the great job you've done," Santa began his traditional year-end speech. Wild cheering from the audience interrupted him.

"They know something," Chris whispered to her.

"They are like this every year," Kristy replied. "They love tradition even more than Dad."

A hush and a frown came from their mother.

"And this year is no different. I confess I would never have made it without a lot of help from all of you." Santa indicated all the gathered elves with a sweep of his arms.

A lump rose in Kristy's throat.

Chris gave her a painful nudge and a thumbs-up.

"Unfortunately, I have to retire and there seem to be no members of my family suitable to assume my duties. So, enjoy your vacations all of you – everyone here is fired! There will be no more Santas on Christmas Eve."

Kristy joined Chris in open-mouthed shock. Silence reigned throughout the hall. Then a curious twittering rose from the elves. Eventually they lost all restraint and burst into raucous laughter. Santa doubled over in hearty ho, ho, hos.

Emma smacked Santa a good one on the arm, then joined in the laughter and said, "You jolly joker."

When the clamor subsided, Santa resumed his annual message.

"My son, Christopher," Santa said loudly and gestured for Chris to join him at the front of the stage. Chris looked like he was ready to barf.

"This young man," Santa declared, giving Chris a huge one-armed hug. He turned him to face the assembled staff, "My son helped to save Santa from near tragedy this Christmas Eve with some of the most marvelous contraptions seen in these parts since my father's time."

"And my wife," Santa continued. He waved Emma forward leaving Kristy standing alone at the back of the stage. "Although I disagree with the way she accomplished it, my darling Emma has made me realize some harsh truths tonight."

There were some quiet whispers and nodding of heads at this point, but Santa pushed on. "And of course, my daughter, Kristine. Without whom, there would have been no Christmas Eve this year.

Santa waved Kristy forward and Emma held both

arms out to enfold her.

"This little girl," Santa said.

"Dad," Kristy scowled.

Santa, ignoring her objection to the word 'little,' continued, "She not only saved Christmas, but she may very well have saved the lives of this Santa and the entire team of reindeer."

A huge cheer rose up from the elves and especially from Chris and Emma. Kristy inflated with the honor of it. Then Santa did a most distressing thing. He took the stocking hat off his head and placed it on Chris's. The room was instantly silent. The elves fidgeted. Chris tried to tear the hat off his head, but Santa held it firm.

"For excellence in invention and the finest toy-making in a generation," Santa announced, "I now introduce you to the North Pole's first official Head Toy Maker!"

While the room filled with shouts and applause, Santa pulled the hat off Chris and placed it on Kristy's head. He pushed it back off her eyes before he continued.

"For the best darn flying this man has ever seen--and I mean ever, for unbelievable courage under extreme distress, for absolute heroism and the strength to get the job done no matter what the obstacles – I introduce you to the new and first ever girl--that is--female Santa Claus in the family!"

The band burst into song again but was quickly drowned out by the shouts, cheers, and whistles of all. Mr. and Mrs. Claus hugged each other as they watched their children come out of shock.

"They'll make a great team," Emma Claus proudly declared.

"That they will," said Kris Claus and he erupted in a final hearty, "Ho, ho, ho!"

"Your dream has come true," Chris said.

"And yours," she answered.

Kristy settled for mutual thumbs-up as Chris pulled away from a hug. They stood together at the front of the stage, grinning and soaking up the applause.

The cheers quieted as their father and mother made their way through the crowd. They squeezed the hands or hugged each elf in turn.

"Do you suppose I should be doing that now?" Kristy asked Chris.

"Probably, but first give me back that hat."

Kristy hung on tight as Chris grabbed the tail of her Santa hat and tried to yank it off.

"Oh, no. It's mine, Dad gave it to me. I am Santa now."

"Well, I am the head toy maker. What do you expect me to wear?"

"How about a funnel?"

Chris let go of Kristy's hat and glared at her.

"We could paint it red and decorate it with fluffy, cotton balls."

Chris took a swipe at her, and Kristy took off running.

"You can blow your hot air out the top," Kristy yelled, then she jumped off the stage. On the dance floor, elves laughed as they parted for her.

"You're getting a little uppity for a little sister," Chris huffed as he chased her through the Christmas crowd.

The word "little" brought her to a quick stop and Chris plowed into her.

"Little sister!" Kristy shouted into his face. "That's

Santa Claus to you, bub. Ho, ho, ho..."

But her voice came out high and small in that big room, causing everyone to pause and look at them.

Kristy looked around. She knew her face was burning red. Chris dropped his hands to his sides in mid grasp. Her parents stopped frowning and smiled.

"I'll have to work on that," she said as loudly and as deeply as she could manage. Then she laughed.

About Atmosphere Press

Atmosphere Press is an independent, full-service publisher for excellent books in all genres and for all audiences. Learn more about what we do at atmospherepress.com.

We encourage you to check out some of Atmosphere's latest releases, which are available at Amazon.com and via order from your local bookstore:

The Gift of Dragons, by Rachel A. Greco

Somewhere Different Now, by Donna Peizer

Taint, by Janet Kelly

The Fantastic Fabricated Life of Lyle Farker, by Kayleigh Marinelli

Abaddon Illusion, by Lindsey Bakken

Tamarack Summers, by Marc Douglass Smith

Dragon Daughter, by Steven Armstrong

Big Beasts, by Patrick Scott

Connie Undone, by Kristine Brown

Katastrophe: The Dramatic Actions of Kat Morgan, by Sylvia M DeSantis

Witches and Vampires, by Brianna White

The Clockwork Witch, by McKenzie P. Odom

The Traveler, by Jennifer Deaver

Spots Before Stripes, by Jonathan Kumar

About the Authors

JAMES AND MAGGIE are a brother and sister writing team from Minnesota, where they still live.

James is an Emmy Award winning videographer, who covers high school, college, and professional sports teams in the Twin Cities. His idea for the book started on one of his family's Christmas trips to Iowa. He says, "You can only listen to so much Christmas music in a four-hour trip." So, he started this story by just making it up to entertain his kids. He thought it might make a good picture book. Wanting some help because of his dyslexia, he brought his notes to his sister, Maggie. She believed the story could be more. Together they dreamed up this adventure at the North Pole and around the world.

Maggie's many jobs ranged from cemetery mowing in college to Board President of a multi-million-dollar non-profit corporation. All her life she has been a storyteller and a voracious reader. This is her first published book.

Printed in the USA
CPSIA information can be obtained
at www.ICGtesting.com
CBHW022035131024
15756CB00010B/71